RUNTS

DANIEL J. VOLPE

Copyright © 2025 Daniel J. Volpe

All rights reserved. No part of this publication may be reproduced, distributed, or transmitted in any form or by any means, including photocopying, recording, or other electronic or mechanical methods, without the prior written permission of the publisher.

Any references to historical events, real people, or real places are used fictitiously. Names, characters, and places are products of the author's imagination.

Front cover art by Nick Justus.

Cover wrap by Don Noble

Edited by Mary Danner.

Printed in the United States of America.

ISBN: 978-1-961758-21-6

For signed copies, visit DJVHORROR.COM

DEDICATION

For Kristopher Triana

RUNTS

DANIEL J. VOLPE

2001.

CHAPTER 1

Kristina Tropiano threw her ass back, taking Clay's cock to the base. She grunted in pleasure as his balls slapped against her wet pussy. The slippery tightness elicited moans from her lover. Together, they found their rhythm, Kristina pushing back as Clay thrust forward. It was a scene they were all too familiar with.

The first time they fucked, after a Clean Ocean seminar, Kristina knew she had the EPA executive in the palm of her hands. Well, not the palm of her hands, but definitely between her legs.

They'd been eyeing each other across the room the entire night, with Clay's wife noticeably missing from the event. Kristina wasn't all that attracted to him, but with his position in the EPA, and her running a chemical company, she knew it wouldn't hurt.

With a head of dirty blonde hair, piercing green eyes, and a set of tits that some people accused her of being fake, Kristina was attractive. At only thirty-two, she was one of the youngest CEOs in her field. She had been immersed in the production world since she was a girl, often shadowing her father and attending all of his meetings.

At first, it was only for free trips around the world, and she didn't have much choice. Since her mother died when she was ten, Kristina and her father were all each other had.

Soon, her attention changed; she no longer found the meetings boring. She'd taken to the industry like a duck to water, seeing the shrewd side of business.

Her father was a perfect, if not corrupt, teacher. He showed her the ropes in his world—where to skimp, and how to maximize profits. But, even with his keen sense of business, the elder Tropiano was set in his ways. He no longer focused on developing new products, but how to maximize the ones he already had.

That didn't sit well with Kristina. She was young and hungry to change the world, for better or for worse.

When her father died, Kristina took over his company and began implementing her business style. She wanted to break free of the stigma her father created, and the first step was renaming the company. The young woman had a level of conceitedness, and she wanted the world to know she was different. And so, KrisCorp was born from the ashes of her father.

Kristina grabbed the headboard of the shitty hotel bed. She arched her back, angling Clay deeper into her body. It wasn't necessary; Clay's cock was, by far, his best feature. It was long, thick, and curved, the best one she'd ever had inside her, even if the man it was attached to wasn't exactly her type.

Clay Briggs was on the wrong side of fifty, with a skinny-fat paunch that hung slightly over his beltline. His gray hair had thinned over the years. He did everything he could to hold it together, from hair growth serums to combovers.

His appearance mattered little to Kristina. It was also one of the main reasons she liked when he fucked her from behind. When he was on top of her, she could smell his cigarette-stinking breath and occasionally feel the drops of sweat that fell on her face. But, from behind, he could be anyone. And more often than not, Kristina fantasized about someone else. Whether it was Marshall, her gay secretary who had a body that was criminally perfect, or even a random guy she'd seen on the street, whenever Clay filled her with his massive cock, it was never attached to him.

As Clay pounded her deeper, she knew her cervix would be sore the next day. It didn't matter. Kristina lived in the moment. At present, she knew they were both getting ready to cum.

Releasing the headboard, Kristina drove her face into the rough pillow and turned her head to the side, her hair draping over her cheek. With her left hand, she reached between her legs and found the swollen nub of her clit.

"Oh fuck, you know I love it when you play with yourself," Clay grunted.

He panted, and Kristina ignored the drops of sweat that landed on her back. Expertly, she rolled the tender morsel of flesh and nerve endings under her soft fingers. If she weren't so fucking horny, she would've taken her time caressing the edges of her clit, not directly on it. But she knew Clay would blow, and once he did, he was as good as useless. She'd end up in the bathroom finishing herself off, but without the pleasure of him inside of her.

She was on a mission to cum before her partner.

Clay pummeled her, driving Kristina's face deeper

into the pillow.

Furiously, she rubbed. Her slit overflowed with their combined wetness, keeping her fingers lubricated. She was almost there.

He fucked her with the ferocity of a man half his age, slamming his shaft into her like he was trying to break her open.

Her orgasm was building, sending her to the point of no return. A wave of pleasure rolled over her, gathering momentum like a sexual tsunami. Her throbbing pussy pulsed around his cock, squeezing him.

"Fuck!" Clay shouted.

Kristina shuddered as she continued to cum. She felt the first shot of Clay's load squirt deep inside of her, then he yanked his cock out with a wet slurp. The next blast hit her in the middle of the back, and the last few dribbles landed on her spread asshole. As her orgasm abated, she collapsed onto the bed.

Clay fell next to her, panting with pleasure and exertion. He put his arm over his face. "Fuck, that was amazing."

Kristina turned her head, aware that the load in her would probably require a shower. She looked at her spent lover, realizing the spunk on her back was dripping. "Um, a little help here."

He pulled his arm from his face and looked at her. His eyes landed on the mess he'd made. "Oh shit, I'm sorry." He rolled over, giving her an unneeded look at his flat ass, and grabbed the box of cheap tissues, then wiped her off and tossed the sodden lump on the floor.

The coolness of the damp spots felt good against her flushed skin when she rolled onto her back. Her breasts hung to the sides, nearly resting on her arms.

She slid back, propping herself up against the headboard. Their fuck session had resulted in it being pulled loose from the wall, but she didn't care. Clay paid for the room, so any damages would be on him, not her.

"Want one?" Clay asked as he grabbed a pack of cigarettes from the nightstand and put a cancer stick into his mouth.

Kristina wasn't a fan of smoking, but when she was younger, she and her boyfriend would fuck each other silly in the back of his old Nissan and light up. She didn't particularly care for it, but he always smoked after sex. She didn't think he liked it either, but they were kids, and smoking after sex was always what the movie stars did.

She put her head back and blew smoke into the air. The taste of the tobacco brought her back to those lustful nights under the stars. A warmth spread between her legs thinking of those times.

"Well, that was certainly fun," Clay said. "Much better than the pathetic sex I have with Louise. When there is sex."

Hearing about Clay's wife didn't precisely get Kristina hot and bothered, but she'd already cum, so he could talk about whatever he wanted. And the secondary reason (the first reason was obviously to fuck like wild animals) was to discuss her business.

When Clay called her to set up the rendezvous, he told her he had some inside information to help her. She figured the 'inside information' was between her legs, but when they met for dinner, Clay had a serious look on his face.

She hadn't made it to where she was without the ability to read people. Something was up, and she always had a clearer mind after she came.

With the carnal necessities taken care of, it was time for business.

As Clay finished his cigarette, he lit another with the dying light of the first one. "As much as I'd like to talk about my pathetic sex life, there's something more serious to discuss."

With the thoughts of her old boyfriend running through her mind, Kristina was feeling horny, and she felt like she could go again. That was if she could coax Clay's cock back to life. For as good as he was, the old man rarely had more than one round in him.

Kristina switched her cigarette into her right hand and let her left fall onto his lap.

There was still rigidity left in his wilting member.

Her lacquered nails gently touched his shaft. Clay didn't stop her, but he was hardly paying attention. Kristina wrapped her fingers around it, letting his cock flop like a Play-Doh snake.

Clay grabbed her hand, thwarting her attempts. "Look, I'd love to fuck again, but we need to talk."

She turned onto her side, letting her breasts collapse into each other. "And what could be more important than me?"

He smashed his cigarette into the ashtray. "Well, it is about you, but it's not good."

Kristina sat up higher, her face scrunched in concern. "Oh? What is it?"

"You're going to be arrested."

Fuck. That is more important than getting off.

CHAPTER 2

"What the fuck are you talking about? I haven't done anything illegal." The lie rolled off her tongue like honey laced with poison—the poison KrisCorp was regularly making.

"These meetups are always fun, and I have feelings for you. And not just the ones between my legs or yours."

The last thing Kristina wanted was a relationship, especially one with a married man who wasn't her type. If it weren't for the hog between his legs and how good he fucked, she would've cut back their visits by a lot.

"Oh, don't give me that, Kris. You and I both know your company makes some nasty shit. And for years, your father has greased the right palms, and you've greased the right pole."

She didn't laugh at his lame joke, even though it was true.

"But after those fucking assholes took down the Twin Towers a few months ago, the Feds have been up everyone's ass, mine included. There are talks of a new department in the works: Homeland Security or something of the sort. Well, after 9/11, the government has been chasing down every lead and company making anything dangerous. A war is coming; that's a fact. I'm sure the killing will be done overseas by kids barely out of high school, but there's another fight starting here. Anything that can be utilized as a weapon is being highly scrutinized. And any company knowingly making unregulated shit, especially those operating outside of the letter of the law, is being watched like an eagle."

Kristina wanted another cigarette. "Let me get another one of those?"

Clay handed her one and took one for himself. He lit them both.

"So, what does this mean? Are the Feds coming after me? But you're the Feds, aren't you?"

"Yes and no. I work for a branch of the government, but even I have overseers. No one operates without scrutiny anymore, and it will only get worse. Someone in KrisCorp has been talking, and their words have found the right ears."

Kristina's smooth flesh rose in goosebumps. She didn't supply terrorists, at least knowingly, but she made some new stuff that had no logical explanation. Of course, she had her top scientists fudge the formulas to make the new stuff appear legitimate. But they knew what they were making. Some of it was bad, but only in certain compound mixtures. Separately, it was harmless, at least from her standpoint. But one of her top scientists created a downright diabolical substance. It didn't have a name, only a designation. SKV092509 was a toxin the world wasn't ready for.

She didn't know who would buy it or what its use

would be, but she knew no good could come from it except for her wallet. It was a deadly compound that would change the face of warfare for years, possibly decades, to come. And she'd get rich off it, just like the arms manufacturers with their tanks, guns, planes, and bombs.

The country was devastated by the attacks in New York, DC, and Pennsylvania, but the war machine was itching to lubricate their weapons with blood. And Kristina was one of them.

"They know about SKV092509, Kris. They know its potential, and they're coming for you. My agency and the FBI will be raiding your main facility in the morning. And when they find the barrels of that shit, it'll be your sweet ass in a sling."

Kristina's mind raced. She could torch the barrels in the incinerator, but she knew the FBI dweebs would head right there and begin swabbing. Any trace of the chemical could spell disaster for KrisCorp and land Kristina in a federal penitentiary. She could even be labeled a terrorist, which would be almost as bad. Her stocks would plummet, and she'd lose everything.

"What can I do? And why didn't you tell me sooner? You had to bust your nut before you could tell me this? I could have started figuring things out." She jumped off the bed and began getting dressed. She put her cigarette in the ashtray without putting it out. A curl of smoke rose from it.

Clay rolled closer to her and ran his fingers down her spine. "Sorry. I had other things on my mind."

She sneered at him over her shoulder. Kristina wanted to tell him to fuck off, but she still needed his help, even if his cock would no longer be of service that evening. "What should I do?" She wrangled her breasts into her bra and clasped it shut.

"You want my opinion? Get rid of it, all of it. I know it has earning potential for you, but you're smart enough to start over, and hopefully, with something that has a slightly more legitimate potential."

"What am I supposed to do with it? I have at least ten barrels of it already made."

Clay raised his hands. "Look, I don't want to know. If I don't know, that means I can't help them. Not that I would, but the Feds have ways of getting information out of people. Do whatever you have to do, but get rid of it and torch the blueprints for the formula. Throw your guys some extra cash and do it now. That's all I can say."

He still hadn't moved from the bed. He lit up another cigarette and began playing with his cock. It rose back to life, swelling with blood.

As pissed and worried as Kristina was, she couldn't help but stare as he stroked himself hard. "Let me make a few calls," she said. "And then you can make this up to me."

Clay grinned at her with tobacco-stained teeth.

Kristina unclasped her bra with one hand as she picked up the phone.

CHAPTER 3

The leaf springs in the van creaked and groaned under the weight of the barrels. Dim headlights cut through the darkness, but there was nothing much for the two occupants to see besides trees.

"So, what does she want us to do with this shit?" Greg asked. He sat in the passenger seat with a cigarette clasped between his fingers; the open window sucked the smoke from the vehicle in a steady stream.

"Don't know," Mitch said from behind the wheel. "She only told me to get rid of it and not tell her where it was."

A steady snowfall drifted from the clouds, dropping flakes on the van's windshield. Mitch hit the wipers, clearing the glass for a moment.

They didn't think it was supposed to snow, but the temperature dropped after driving higher into the mountains. What started as rain slowly turned into a mix and then full-on snow. The roads were covered with a light dusting, but they would only get worse the farther they drove.

"What kinda shit is it that we had to get called out in the middle of the night?" Greg asked.

He flicked the cigarette butt from the van and rolled the window up. Even with gloves on, his hands were still cold. Greg turned the dial for the heat, but the old van didn't have the best equipment.

Slightly-warm air blew out of the vents, but it was better than nothing.

Mitch shrugged. "Bad shit, I assume. You know what kind of stuff they make. And since this was a rush job, it's gotta be the worst of the worst."

Greg scoffed. "That's reassuring." He rubbed his hands. They'd regained enough warmth for him to justify another smoke. He lit up and cracked the window again. "It's a good thing she's paying us well." Greg looked over at his partner, who focused on the worsening road. "I'd settle for less pay if I could get a taste of her ass."

"Hell yeah. I bet her turd cutter is as sweet as honey. Although there's a rumor she doesn't like her ass eaten." Mitch laughed.

"Bullshit. I've never met a broad that doesn't like a tongue in the shitter."

"I don't know. That's the word on the street." Mitch gasped as the van slid.

He took his foot from the gas and resisted slamming the brakes. He'd been driving long enough to know that would spell disaster for both of them. The last thing he needed was to get into an accident, especially in the middle of nowhere. And with a load of dangerous chemicals on board, it would be even worse.

"Damn, these roads are shit," Greg stated the obvious. "Where do you want to dump this stuff? I don't feel like getting stranded out here. I haven't seen a town in miles. Not since we passed that podunk town, if it could even be called a town, miles back."

The snow fell faster and harder.

Mitch turned the wipers up a notch, and the twin blades raced back and forth, trying to keep the glass clear. "Yeah, I don't like this shit either. It's only gonna get worse the further we drive." He slowed down in an attempt to read a snowy sign. "Shadow Bear Creek, two miles," he said.

"Perfect. Let's see if there's an access road that's semi-decent and dump this shit. If this snow keeps up, anything we dump will be buried for the winter, especially if we throw it in the water. I'm sure it's not that deep, but hopefully enough to keep these fucking barrels covered for a while."

"Sounds like a plan."

The snow worsened, but Mitch found the pull-off leading to the creek.

"It looks sketchy to me," Greg said as Mitch slowed the van to a halt. "But it's our only shot."

Mitch nodded as he carefully drove the van toward the water.

The van slipped, but the tires found enough purchase on the soft ground underneath the blanket of snow.

Slowly, he inched forward until they saw the black snake of the stream. They left the van running as they got out.

Greg took a massive flashlight from the glovebox and turned it on. It wasn't the brightest, but it was enough for them to see. "Damn, that's a hell of a creek."

Shadow Bear was a creek only in name. It ran

calmly, signifying the water was deep.

"Okay, let's dump this and get the fuck out of here."

They unloaded the barrels, carefully opening each one before pushing them out into the water.

PRESENT DAY

CHAPTER 4

The Toyota had little room, but the four passengers made it work. It wasn't Jackson's first car of choice, but his part-time job and college didn't provide him with many options. When he did work, his hourly rate was just enough to cover his meager expenses, let alone spring for a new car, so when he saw the older Corolla for sale, he knew it was the perfect vehicle to fit his lifestyle.

After college, when he could find a stable job, he'd upgrade his ride. But for now, the old, Japanese car suited him just fine.

His friends made fun of the sedan, which was riddled with spots of rust, but then again, they didn't complain when he offered to drive. Even his shitbox beat taking the bus.

Skylar would also break his balls about the car, but he didn't expect anything less from his younger sister. Their birthdays landed only thirteen months apart. Apparently, no one told their parents to practice safe sex after Jackson was born.

"I hope it doesn't snow the entire time," Trenton said from the front passenger seat. "I'm trying to get home to my bed before my dad sells it. You know he's itching to move as soon as he can." He rested his head against the window and pulled his cell phone from his pocket. With a few taps on the screen, he pulled up his weather app. "Ugh, this shit is only gonna get worse."

Jackson said a small prayer when he saw the new tires his car had come equipped with. He didn't notice much during the summer, but now that he was driving into a blizzard, he was thankful for the fresh rubber. Even though the car was light, the combination of good tires and a manual transmission made driving in the snow much safer.

Emmett leaned forward from the backseat. "You know your dad won't go through your room. He's afraid of what he'll find."

Trenton slipped his phone into his pocket and laughed. "Ain't that the truth. When I came out to them, my dad didn't say anything. And I mean *anything*. He pretty much ignored it but hasn't given me shit one way or another. I think he just put it from his mind, and that's fine. Even when I've brought guys home, he always called them my 'friends.'" He laughed again. "You all are my friends, and I've never gotten my dick sucked by any of you."

"Jesus, Trent. I could go without the visuals here," Emmett said.

Trenton laughed harder. "Honey, I could give you visuals to make your head spin. And maybe get you a little hard." He blew a kiss to his friend. "Maybe I could even turn you too."

Emmett sat back in his seat. "Sorry, princess, I'm as straight as an arrow." He looked over at Skylar, who was sitting next to him.

She was looking out of her window, seemingly ignoring the banter.

"Hmm, that's what they all say. But every straight guy has a little gay in him, they just don't accept it. You've never really gotten head until you get it from a hot guy."

"Come on, Trent," Jackson said. "I've had plenty of great blowjobs. The girls at college know their way around a cock."

"Um, your sister is here, asshole," Skylar chimed in, joining the conversation. "Can we not talk about sucking dick or fucking for two seconds. God, you all are perverts."

Trent pulled his visor down and opened the small mirror, looking back at Skylar. "Honey, I'm sure you've had a dick or two at college. Don't be a prude because your brother is in the car. Hell, he sure as shit isn't." Trent's eyes flashed over to Emmett to see his reaction.

Emmett blushed and looked at Skylar from the corner of his eye.

The night he and Skylar finally had sex was one of the best nights of his life. His college sex life wasn't much to be desired, and for good reason. Emmett was never what most women called attractive. His ears were just slightly too big, as was his nose. And, as one girl told him, "There's just something off with your face."

He tried what he could, short of surgery, to fix his face, but nothing helped. The few times he did hook up with a girl, it hadn't gone well.

No matter how much he fought it, he couldn't get Skylar out of his mind. He loved her, but couldn't gauge how she felt about him. Ever since they were kids, he'd had a crush on her. Their young love seemed to swap back and forth, at least in Emmett's mind, from year to year, but as they grew older, he realized that was a lie.

When he finally gathered the nerve to ask her out in their junior year of high school, Skylar quickly told him she didn't want to ruin their friendship.

Emmett was crushed. All the fantasies about his future were dashed away in an instant.

Soon after the brutal rejection, Skylar began dating Derek. Seeing the two of them in the hallway had nearly crippled Emmett. He'd never walked as fast as he had the first time he saw his love make out with someone else.

Skylar and Derek dated until senior year. She even lost her virginity to him, but that didn't stop his dick from wandering. When she caught him fucking Charlotte in his car just before graduation, she'd been devastated.

Emmett felt terrible for her, but knew it was his chance. He took his shot over the summer, leaning in for their first kiss. She stopped him, crushing his dreams once again, and leaving him in a puddle of emotions.

"Look, I like you, Emmett, I really do. But I'm not ready for another relationship right now, especially with us going away in a few months to college."

He wanted to remind her they'd be headed to the same school, and it was only the start of a relationship that would end in their marriage. He knew it and just had to convince her, but he fought back the torrent of emotions and respected her wishes.

The four of them spent the rest of the summer

together, amid the brewing sexual tension between Skylar and Emmett. And then, during their first weekend at school, it finally happened.

Skylar called him at two in the morning crying. She was a blabbering mess, saying how Derek kept calling her and telling her he'd made a mistake and wanted her back. She was torn and didn't know what to do.

Emmett did his best to console her, but deep down, he wanted to tell her to forget her ex, that much better things awaited her if she only gave them a chance.

After a half hour of talking, he calmed her down. Emmett was about to fall asleep when a light knock on his door roused him.

It was Skylar, half drunk in a hoodie and sweats. Her eyes were red and her hair a mess, but to him, she looked perfect.

He didn't hesitate, kissing her on the threshold of his tiny dorm room. And this time, she didn't push him away. Within seconds, they were both naked. Their mouths seemingly never separated as they fucked. It wasn't slow or special, like Emmett thought it would be. No, it was feral. Years of repressed sexual tension poured into each other.

Emmett slept like a baby that night, but Skylar was gone when he awoke in the morning. The only remnant of her was her scent on his pillow. He wanted to call her, but figured she needed space. He couldn't fumble things with her again.

When he saw her in their Monday morning Biology class, Skylar acted like nothing happened. He thought her chipper mood was due to their blossoming relationship, but it wasn't. She was happy she'd passed her first math quiz and nothing else.

And in an instant, their one-night stand became just that—nothing more than a cheap thrill.

Returning to the present, Emmett snapped out of the confusion of their relationship. He wanted to get the conversation off sex. The last thing he wanted to hear was about Skylar and other guys. "Do you think they will have the Christmas village again?"

"Knowing our town, absolutely. You know they're all about traditions and shit. Our little slice of mundane is as American as apple pie. Flags flying, crosses hanging, and enough dirty laundry to keep anyone busy." Trenton checked his profile in the mirror before flipping the visor up.

The snow continued to fall heavy and thick, covering the lines of the road.

Jackson slowed the car by downshifting instead of hitting the brakes. "Fuck," he said, guiding the car around a slight bend.

"What?" Skylar asked, looking out of the windshield. "I don't see anything."

"Not in the road," Jackson said. He pointed at his phone attached to the dashboard and displayed the GPS. "That."

The road they traveled had a red line with a warning emblem over it. Other routes were outlined in blue, but they were nowhere near where they needed to be. Their arrival time had increased by three hours and the mileage by over one-hundred-fifty.

"Fuck. My dad is definitely throwing my shit away," Trenton said.

***

The flashing lights of a police car reflected off the

falling snow in the distance.

"And there's the fucking closure," Jackson said. Gently, he applied the brakes as he downshifted.

The cop jumped out of his car, not thrilled to be in the snow. "Road's closed," he said.

Snowflakes landed on his dark jacket. He stuffed his hands in his pockets and stamped his feet. "The snow knocked down a few trees and telephone poles, so there's no getting through."

"I told you we should've taken the interstate," Emmett said. "But we *had* to go the scenic route through the mountains."

"We can't predict the weather," Skylar snapped.

Emmett sat back, scalded. He'd forgotten the scenic route had initially been her idea. With his foot firmly in his mouth, he shut up and listened to the cop.

"You can go around me for about a mile. There will be a road on your right. Take that for a few miles and you'll hit the town of Braxton right along the Shadow Bear Creek. It's not much, but it has a restaurant or two and a motel."

"Oh no thanks, we need to get home," Trenton said, leaning over Jackson.

The cop looked into the car and then back to the road. "How far are you all heading?"

"Farther north to Ashmore."

"Ashmore, New York? You aren't gonna make it, especially in this thing," the cop said, gesturing to the Toyota. "Hell, even if you had a 4x4, it would be tricky. These mountain roads aren't going to be plowed until the storm stops, and if we get the amount of snow they're predicting, that won't be for a while. Your best bet is to slowly make your way to Braxton and spend the night. By the morning, or possibly the afternoon, the roads will be good enough to get you going again."

"Damn. Well, thank you," Jackson said as he rolled the window up.

The cop brushed the snow from his jacket and returned to his running cruiser.

"What do you guys think?"

"A hotel room isn't really in the budget, but crashing in the middle of nowhere doesn't sound like a great time either," Skylar said.

"Yeah, I agree," Emmett responded.

"Of course you do, hun." Trenton pulled a vape from his small bag. He breathed deep and let out a cloud of fruity-smelling vapor. "Anyone else? I promise it's only nicotine and not weed."

Jackson took it and puffed, letting the chemicals calm his mind.

Emmett and Skylar declined.

The snow fell harder, and the car shook from the blowing wind.

"Look, I think it's the best bet. We find a place to stay for the night, get a hot meal, and maybe some drinks. I doubt the local bar will notice our fake IDs. And if they do, I know we have a few bottles stashed in our bags between the four of us," Jackson said.

The other three grumbled, knowing he was right.

"Em, what do you think?"

Emmett knew what he was thinking: snowed in with Skylar in a little mountain motel? It was pretty much perfect. He wanted to be home as bad as the others, but if he could rekindle the spark between them, he would. "It's probably the safest bet. This little car is good, but this snow is no joke. And with the temps dropping, getting stranded somewhere would fucking suck."

In the rearview, Jackson spotted approaching headlights.

A large pickup was barreling down the snow-covered road like dry pavement.

Jackson put his car in first gear and moved to the side of the road, letting the truck blow by.

It shot up a rooster tail of powder as the ass end of it slid around the police car.

"What an asshole," Trent said. "Welcome to the country, big trucks and small dicks."

Jackson followed the truck, sticking to its grooves in the snow. In the distance, he saw the big vehicle hit its right blinker, heading toward Braxton.

CHAPTER 5

Janice had given birth before, but she knew something about this time was different. Since the day she conceived, she felt something was *off*. The baby moved normally, and her cravings weren't different from the other pregnancies, but she knew.

Braxton had a curse on it, something that had been around for decades. Since the unmarked barrels had been found in the Shadow Bear Creek after the spring thaw almost twenty-five years ago, things hadn't been right.

It started with Eileen and Scott's little boy in the fall of '02. It was her first pregnancy, and she was happy, even though Scott had refused to get married. Things like that happened worldwide, but at least Scott agreed to stick around and not bail on his pregnant girlfriend. Even if he wanted to, most residents of Braxton were lifers, not venturing far from the mountain town.

When Eileen's baby came out with a head like a potato—misshapen and lumpy—she'd cried for a week. And then, the baby was gone. No one knew what happened to him; he was just gone.

In the winter of that year, she was found hanging in an old barn on her father's defunct farm with a suicide note that just said, ***I'm sorry.***

Since that day, many of Braxton's children were born with horrific mutations. Some mothers and fathers were lucky, having perfectly normal offspring, but on occasion, they were born into the world as an abomination—missing limbs, disgusting sores, club feet, organs on the outside of their bodies, you name it.

The night Beau blew his load into Janice, she knew she was pregnant. And she knew it wasn't normal.

Janice lay in a puddle of sweat. Her sheets were soaked, and the mattress would require days to dry. She sat up against the wall. Her dark hair was wet and matted to her head. The pimples she'd grown during pregnancy were angry and red, weeping with burst white heads. She was nude, as it was the only way she could keep her body temperature down.

The bedroom window was open, letting the snow pile on the floor.

Her stomach was oblong and distended, her belly button completely flat. Towels were piled up under her ass in preparation for the birth. She didn't think they were going to be enough.

Beau sat in the chair next to her, holding his wife's hand. He wasn't a big man and felt like his wife was going to break the small bones with every contraction.

"I-I can't fucking do this," Janice yelled.

Another contraction began building, and the urge to push grew unbearable.

Beau stood and wiped her sweaty face. The cloth bore streaks of blood from the broken pimples, but he did his best not to hurt her. "You can do it, babe. You have to. For the baby."

"This baby is going to be a monster. A fucking curse of Braxton."

"Shh, don't talk like that. This baby will be healthy and happy like its brother and sister."

Cartoons played loudly in the living room, a vain attempt to keep their other kids from hearing screams from the bedroom.

Typically, Beau would've driven his wife to the hospital to give birth, but the nearest one was over an hour away on a good day. It would have taken him triple that time to get her there in the blizzard. Their SUV was equipped with big tires and four-wheel-drive, but he couldn't risk it, especially panicked. So, having the child at home was the only option. He just prayed the kid was normal.

Janice screamed and grunted, pushing with all her strength.

Beau looked at the hairy, bloody mess that was his wife's vagina.

Something moved.

"That's it. The baby is coming. I can see the head." He watched her other births, not minding the gore, and sometimes shit, that came from his wife. Beau loved her, and the miracle of life was extraordinary.

His buddies told him watching her give birth would ruin pussy for him, but it hadn't. Beau still fucked and ate her like it was nothing.

The contraction passed, and the head sucked back into her body. "On the next contraction, I'm going to help you, okay?"

Janice looked at him and nodded. "Just get this fucking thing out of me!"

He ran out of the room and into the bathroom to wash his hands and forearms. He knew it wasn't perfect, but it was better than nothing.

When he entered the room again, Janice was pushing. "Oh shit," he said, moving between his wife's legs.

The head was nearly out with the baby face down.

He grabbed it under the chin and knew his wife's suspicions were confirmed. Even though Beau couldn't see his child's face, he knew it was wrong. Very wrong. "Push."

Janice bore down. Feces and amniotic fluid gushed from her.

Beau pulled gently on the baby, doing his best to work it free from the birth canal.

One shoulder popped out, then the other. In a tidal wave of blood and fluid, the baby was born.

Beau held in his scream when he saw his offspring.

The baby's face was a mess. A cleft ran from its crying mouth, splitting the nose. It had no ears, only holes in its head. The left arm ended at the shoulder, with four nubby fingers sticking out like little sausages. Its left leg wasn't much better. It was stunted and ended in a gnarled club.

A wave of relief washed over Janice's face when the pressure finally left her body, but when her husband laid the pink baby on her chest, that all changed. Janice screamed at seeing the abomination she'd brought into the world.

Beau looked at it stunned, his face blank.

Kill it. It's the right thing to do. A twist of the neck to put it out of its misery, and ours. You wouldn't be the first. A quick burial, or even a garbage bag, would be mercy rather than a life of misery.

Janice's screams turned to whimpers as she cradled her mutated daughter. She kissed the wet crown of the baby's head.

***

How could she love a monster? Janice felt her soul scream as she wrapped the baby in a blanket. It was just as she feared: the curse of Braxton lived on, and she was a recipient of it. Her husband looked at her in a way she'd never seen before. When their other two kids were born, pride lit his face. Now, he wore a look of disgust, but there was something else there, something dark.

"W-what are you thinking? Don't lie to me, Beau."

Beau sat in the chair next to the bed. His Adam's apple bobbed as he swallowed hard.

She could tell he was doing his best to come up with an answer.

"We need to get rid of *it*."

He didn't say 'her' or 'the baby'; it was immediately a thing to him—something evil and ruined. "Give it to me. I'll take care of it." He stood and put his arms out.

Janice clutched the baby to her chest. She wasn't crying anymore.

The baby was silent, just looking around in wonder. Her cleft mouth was puckering like a fish out of water.

Instinctively, Janice brought its deformed mouth to her swollen breast. The baby did its best to find her leaking nipple, but with the shape of her mouth, it was nearly impossible.

"Beau, no. We can't; she's ours." Janice lifted her

breast, trying to get her nipple in the baby's mouth. She'd never had a baby feed so early after birth, but her instincts were something she couldn't deny.

"Oh, no?" Beau spat with scorn. "And what the fuck are we supposed to do? I hardly make enough to keep us afloat as it is. This-this freak," he yelled, "is going to need special attention. Doctors, Janice, and not that fucking quack in town, like *real* doctors. And who the hell knows what's wrong with its brain? It'll probably be a retard, drooling and shitting on itself forever. Do you want to deal with that? How the hell would you be able to go to work when you have a child that needs constant attention? We get away with it now because Sherry can watch the other two without a problem. But do you think she'd going to wipe this monster's ass all day? Or carry it around?"

Janice felt her soul shatter. She hated Beau at that moment, and deep down, she hated herself. She knew her husband was right, but she loathed the idea. They'd be ruined caring for the baby. It was no life for either of them. The baby might not even live, which she, sadly, thought was a blessing.

"What about *her?* She'd take the baby. She's done it before."

Beau rubbed his face, leaving streaks of blood on his stubble. He didn't seem to notice his soiled fingers. After a long pause, he spoke. "You think giving the baby to that witch is better than a quick death? Do you want that? To let her raise this thing with the other creatures in her cabin? Those fucking things would probably eat it before we left."

Milk ran down between Janice's breasts as the baby gnawed on her sore nipple. Giving her baby up wasn't something she wanted, but what other option did they have? Raise the child and destroy their small family? Let her husband murder the infant? No, that wasn't an option either. She couldn't let that happen.

"She'll take her in, I know it."

"Give it to me. Let's be done with this now." Beau said, holding his hands out again.

Clutching the infant to her, Janice wept. "No, please, let her take the baby. I couldn't live with myself if you did that."

They all knew the story of Eileen. Janice didn't know if she'd truly kill herself, but with the wave of post-partum emotions, she couldn't be certain.

Beau huffed and shook his head. "Fine. I'll help clean you up, but then we're going. I don't want this thing under my roof for a second longer than necessary."

Janice smiled a pained smile. It wasn't the perfect outcome, but it was better than death, that was certain. "Find the old pump. I can't leave her without something to eat."

CHAPTER 6

For as long as Leona could remember, she'd been called Grammy. Even when she was a girl, she had motherly qualities about her. The other kids would make fun of her when she wouldn't participate in fear of getting in trouble. They would cause havoc, drinking and breaking shit, and Leona would hang back. Soon, the other kids started telling her she was a mother hen. But then, one of them said she was even worse—not a mother, but a grandmother. So, the name Grammy was born. Leona initially hated it, but soon adopted it as her own, taking the power away from the bullies.

Grammy was no longer a little girl. She wasn't even a young woman anymore. Her gray hair was in a loose bun as she stirred the large pot of stew at the kitchen counter. It wasn't much of a stew, more like a weak soup, but it was all she had.

She and her children had to eat, and with the winter in full effect, food was getting scarce.

Her house was handed down through generations, with each family member seemingly adding an outbuilding. It was originally used as a hunting cabin, but one of her ancestors had added to it, building a few more crude rooms off the back.

Her grandpappy built two small sheds, and her father added one more. Originally, they were used to house firewood, which provided most of the heat for the house.

Her father's plan with his building was to raise chickens, which he did for a few years. But when his birds were decimated by a poor winter and predators, he abandoned the idea. Over the years, the buildings were turned into rough bunkhouses.

Grammy may have been the last blood relative left, but her family was far from small. Known for her charity and kindness, the townspeople of Braxton would often leave their problems with her, though some didn't quite approve of her, frequently calling her a witch.

The kids in the town had become worse since she was a girl. Rumors flew about the old woman on the edge of town, and with that, came fear.

She'd often been the victim of vandalism, and not only by children, so when she saw the headlights of an SUV bounding down her long driveway, she was immediately on guard. The big vehicle pushed through the snow, crunching over it with ease.

Grammy put down her wooden spoon and looked as it approached.

Heavy footsteps echoed on the wooden floor next to her. She didn't move or look back; she knew it was Hammer, her first 'child.'

His shadow dwarfed the old woman, but then again, Hammer dwarfed everyone. His deformed hand reached past her, pulling the meat cleaver from the butcher's block.

"Who the fuck is that?" Hammer asked.

Grammy turned and placed a hand on his muscled arm. It was the size of a log and corded with powerful meat.

Hammer stood at nearly seven feet. In any other place and time, he would've been a pro athlete or a strongman. But Braxton had cursed him, as it had with the rest of her 'children.' Hammer's face was a misshapen lump of flesh and hair. His left eye was deep-set in his wrinkled skin. The right one drooped and sat inches lower than the left. His mouth was askew, full of crooked teeth.

The overalls he wore were the biggest ones Leona could find, and they only came to just below his knee. And it was a good thing they did. He didn't get the name Hammer from his height, but from what was between his legs. Even without looking at his crotch, Grammy could see the outline of his penis. It looked like it belonged to a thoroughbred, not a man.

She let all her 'children,' the Runts, as they'd taken to calling themselves, name each other. It was never her plan, just something that happened, but it gave them a sense of belonging. Losing the names they'd been born with, if they had one, and getting a new one made them a part of the family.

Grammy hadn't chosen her name either, so it only seemed fitting for her to let them do the same. She couldn't say she agreed with some of their names, but it was them. It was who they were.

"Be still, child," she said.

Hammer's muscles rippled under his tight shirt, but he didn't move. His deformed eyes only watched. His hand adjusted on the cleaver, which looked like a toy in his paw.

"I know that truck."

The large vehicle slowed to a stop not far from the house. She couldn't make out the occupants, but was pretty sure she knew who they were.

Beau and Janice Cooper weren't bad people, at least Janice wasn't. When Grammy scrounged some cash together, she'd often walk to town, grabbing meager groceries.

Janice was a cashier in the only grocery store in Braxton. Grammy didn't know if it was fear or kindness, but if she left the store with a few unpaid items, Janice never raised the alarm or said a thing. Even if it was fear, she didn't care; the woman took care of her. The last time Grammy had seen her, Janice's baby bump was starting to grow.

"Go get your siblings. We might have a new addition to the family."

Hammer looked down at her. The lantern light reflected off his greasy hair and made his eyes twinkle. "Another one? We can hardly feed ourselves, let alone another mouth."

Grammy nodded but didn't speak.

The townspeople had been generous when she'd taken in the first of the Runts. They often dropped off food or supplies as a thank you for settling their problems. But not all of her Runts were so well behaved. Mischief would happen in town, and sometimes an assault or rape. It would seldom be her children, but they were easy scapegoats for the derelicts of Braxton. Soon, the rumors grew, and the people began to fear the old woman and deformed kids in the woods. Donations slowed and finally stopped. And then, the vandalism started.

Hammer had only been ten when he caught a few of the local kids driving their trucks through one of the few fertile fields on the property. Even at ten, Hammer was the size of a large man and had the temper of a drunk one.

A farm boy, who Grammy later found out was the son of Donny Shield, took a swing at Hammer. That didn't go over well, ending with the younger boy nearly breaking Hunter Shield's arm in two. Of course, Hunter lied about the attack, getting his buddies to say they were attacked by the freakish boy in town.

Grammy didn't want trouble, especially with Donny. He was rumored to own half of Braxton and employed many people in town. When Donny came to her house with a few other rough-looking men, Grammy was scared. She wasn't worried about what they'd do to her, but what her children would do to the men.

Once she showed Donny the gouge marks on her property, he seemed to settle, at least on the inside. On the outside, he was still a tempest but had to save face in front of the men.

Grammy would've bet everything she owned that Hunter's truck was mud splattered from driving through her field.

Donny left, but told the old woman he was watching her.

Even with Donny's disapproval, it didn't stop the townsfolk from bringing their cursed children to her. To them, they were a burden, but to her, they were special, each and every one of them.

"I didn't ask your opinion; I told you to do something. Now git."

Hammer put the cleaver down and looked at his

feet in shame. "Yes, Grammy." He clunked away into the house.

Grammy knew he was right. The winter was already starting rough, with heavy snow blanketing everything. Her food stores ran low, and her Runts weren't the best hunters. She set a few traps around the property, but the snow would render them obsolete unless she pulled them and reset them somewhere else.

Babies were another problem all in their own right. They didn't eat solid food like the others; they needed milk, diapers, and warmth, three things Grammy didn't have. She could sew together a few diapers, but milk wasn't an option.

Janice and Beau hadn't exited their vehicle yet. Grammy couldn't see them through the dark glass, but knew they were watching her through the window. She half expected them to drive away and deal with the baby on their own. They wouldn't be the first parents to leave a baby in the woods screaming from a deformed mouth until a hungry animal found them.

Part of Grammy wanted them to put the car in reverse and drive out of her life. But the part of her that loved and cherished them all couldn't stand the thought. She gave her stew one final stir and grabbed her coat and boots. If the Coopers wouldn't come to her, she'd go to them.

It was almost supper time, and the Runts were getting hungry.

CHAPTER 7

The Corolla slid into what Jackson believed to be a parking space in front of the motel. They all let out a sigh of relief and looked at each other.

"Well, that certainly sucked dick," Jackson said.

"Nah, sucking dick is a great time. That was like listening to my grandmother talk about religion," Trenton said. "And as much as I love you guys, I need to get the hell out of this car." He opened his door as a gust of icy wind blew, showering the car's interior with snowflakes.

"Jesus Christ," Skylar said as the cold wind chilled her.

Jackson killed the engine, then the four of them ran toward the motel lobby.

The motel wasn't much, but it was shelter from the storm, and they were grateful for that. It was two stories and looked old, with twelve rooms—six up and six down. A small lobby sat in the middle of the building with the soft glow of incandescent light spilling into the snow.

The cop wasn't lying when he said Braxton was a small town.

On their slow drive in, they saw rows of houses scattered into the hills. One traffic light blew in the wind, set to blink amber. A few shops had their lights off, and the lone gas station was dimly lit and looked closed. The only places that appeared open were a restaurant, The Shield, and the motel, aptly named The Sword Inn.

Emmett opened the door to the motel, letting Skylar and the others go before him.

The sound of a TV could be heard, but none could see where it was coming from.

A man sat behind the front desk, which was the only object in the room besides a few fake plants and a flyer rack. "You folks need some rooms?" he asked.

Jackson approached the counter, snow melting from his jacket creating a puddle on the floor.

The man was older, but not quite old, and sat on an office chair that had seen better days. His short haircut screamed former military, as did the gray mustache. The rest of his face was clean-shaven, like he'd taken care of the stubble just before they walked in. His face glowed from the TV, which must've been tucked behind the counter; explosions came from the speakers, and John Wayne's voice followed shortly after.

The clerk stood, not taking his eyes off the TV for a moment before addressing them. A gold tag clung to his shirt, displaying his name as *Donald S.* He grabbed the remote and lowered the volume on the TV.

Donald looked at all of them, and his lip rose in a slight sneer as his eyes settled on Trent. He reached into his shirt pocket and pulled out a gnawed toothpick, sticking it into the corner of his mouth. A smile rose on his lips, lighting up his ice-blue eyes.

"Rooms are two hundred a night."

"What? Two hundred for this place?" Trent burst out, asking. "That's a fucking robbery."

Emmett grabbed his arm and pulled him back before he jumped the counter. "Shut up," he hissed.

"Yup. You kids have never heard of supply and demand. Well, this is the only motel within a hundred miles or so, and I don't think that Jap shitbox is gonna get you much further. So, you see, I make the rules, and you make the payment. Simple. Oh, and it's cash only. No plastic here."

"Motherfucker," Trenton grumbled, which elicited a bigger smile from Donald. "Why is everyone named Donald a fucking asshole?" he asked to no one in particular.

"If Twinkle Toes doesn't shut his fucking mouth, the price is gonna go up to three hundred."

"No, no, two hundred is just fine," Skylar said, stepping beside her brother. Her skin crawled as Donald's eyes looked over every inch of her. Even fully clothed and in a jacket, she felt violated.

"Ah, there's a little common sense. Thank you, young lady." His eyes lingered on her chest.

"We'll take one room, preferably with two beds." She paused briefly and did her best not to roll her eyes. "Please." She opened her purse and removed the cash, handing it to Donald.

He grabbed the money, making it a point to caress her hand as he did, then dropped the money on the counter and locked eyes with her. Donald backed up and took the toothpick from his mouth, replacing it with a cigarette. He lit it with a zippo with a military-looking emblem on it. The smoke rose into his face but didn't bother him. "See, a little common courtesy goes a long way."

Trenton made it a point to cough loudly, but said nothing.

Donald pinched the cigarette between his forefinger and middle finger, looking at it. "I know, terrible habit, right? But I can't give the damn things up and these toothpicks don't do shit." He sat back down and clicked away on what sounded like an ancient computer.

There was a jingle of keys before Donald tossed a physical key with a large tag bearing a *6* on it. "Room six, end of the building that way." He pointed to his right. "We don't have room service, and the maid is off. But, if you folks are hungry, The Shield is still open, but that's about it. I wouldn't eat from the vending machine outside. That shit was in there from before I was born. Have a pleasant night and thanks for staying at The Sword Inn."

Jackson grabbed the key, and back out into the storm they went.

CHAPTER 8

Janice clutched the baby to her breast. The newborn did her best to suckle, but it was impossible with the extreme cleft. Still, the baby didn't cry. She hadn't cried since she'd been born.

The same couldn't be said for Janice. Since she and Beau decided to give the baby up to Grammy, she hadn't stopped crying. They both knew it was the correct answer, at least, that's what Beau said. And in his rage at producing what he called a freak, he doubled down on his threat to kill the newborn.

"It would be a mercy, Jan, for it and us." *It*, he couldn't even call his daughter *she*.

As much as Janice tried to vilify him, she was just as guilty. She wouldn't even give the baby a name. The only things she'd done since her daughter was born were cry and pump breastmilk.

Luckily for her and the baby, her breasts were already full and producing more than expected. Janice pumped until she was sore, filling small bags with the milk. She didn't know how long the small supply would last, but it was no longer her problem after they drove away.

A fresh current of tears ran down her face as she cooed to her baby. It wasn't to silence the child, who was still silent, just looking at the world. It was to help still the guilt in her heart.

Even with the deformation, there was something adorable about the baby. Janice already loved her and always would. But she knew Beau. Sometimes, he was all talk, but this was different—this would affect the rest of them.

Her other two children would be teased for having a freak for a sister. The other people in town would shun them, knowing what the right decision was. They weren't the first family in Braxton to drive out into the woods. And they wouldn't have been the first to dash the head of a baby with a hammer, dropping it in an unmarked grave.

The big SUV rumbled; the dashboard lights provided the only illumination source.

A lighter flicked as Beau lit a cigarette. The orange flame lit his face, making him look like the devil.

He is the devil. But I'm right here, so I must be in Hell with him. "I-I don't know if I can do this," Janice croaked.

She gently bounced the baby. The saliva from the nursing attempts left Janice's breast wet and cold. She adjusted the newborn and pulled her shirt back over her damp chest. Her heart was cold, and not just from the moisture. She wanted to tell Beau not to smoke around the baby, but for what? A little secondhand smoke would hardly do anything. And in moments, she would no longer be their problem.

Beau turned and looked at her. He picked an errant

piece of tobacco from his mouth and flicked it into the darkness. "Janice, we talked about this. If I turn this car around, that-that...*thing* is dead. Is that what you want? Huh? For me to smash its head and leave it for the coyotes and foxes? No, you don't. And neither do I. I'm not a killer, but that would be the merciful thing to do, for *it* and us." He pulled hard on his smoke, the glowing tip wavering.

Janice let out a sob and clutched the wiggling baby tighter.

"Come on, let's get this over with." He opened the door, letting the blustery cold swirl into the cab.

Janice looked at the deformed face of her child. "I'm so sorry, little one." She kissed the misshapen forehead between the crooked eyes and opened the door.

***

Grammy bundled up and watched. She'd seen this before but couldn't decide for them. As badly as she wanted to save every child, many cars turned around before surrendering their offspring to her. She knew what that meant. After they'd driven away with the child, she often heard the telltale howls and cries of coyotes as they fed. Each one broke her heart. A new child was always a challenge, especially a baby, but she didn't have it in her heart to turn them away.

The SUV doors opened, and she breathed a sigh of relief. That was step one.

Grammy walked out into the cold of the night. The snow bit at her wrinkled face, but she held firm, watching them. Her boots crunched in the snow as she walked toward the SUV, but she stopped short. It was essential to let them come to her. She knew the stories about her and her Runts and couldn't seem eager.

Janice stepped forward with the baby in her arms. She had a plastic shopping bag full of something draped over her wrist. "Please, help our baby." She walked closer to Grammy, but kept the baby pressed against her chest, shielding the child from the weather. Or was it to feel the warmth of the small body for a last time?

Grammy looked down at the swaddled child. Her face was a mess, one of the worst ones she'd seen. *Is the curse getting stronger?* She pushed the thought from her mind.

It wasn't a curse; they had been poisoned. The children she took in weren't monsters, regardless of what people said. They were victims of greed and fear.

Grammy held out her arms to accept the baby.

Janice shuddered and clutched her tighter, causing the newborn to whimper and cry.

Beau stepped up next to his wife. "Give her the baby." He dropped his cigarette into the snow; it died with a hiss.

Janice looked at her husband. Streaks of tears froze on her pale skin. "I-I—"

"Yes, you can, Jan. Just do it."

Janice nodded and kissed the baby on the head.

"Shh, little one, don't cry. You're home now," Grammy said. She smiled, showing the gaps in her mouth where some of her teeth had been. "You know, this is another mouth to feed. And I have plenty of other hungry children."

Nearly forgetting the bag on her arm, Janice pulled it from her wrist. "Here. This is all I could pump in the short time I had."

Adjusting the swaddled infant, Grammy took the bag. She looked in and was surprised. Cut with a little goat's milk, the breastmilk would last a while. Not long enough, but it was better than nothing.

"I'll bring you more, honest."

Grammy nodded as the lie rolled off Janice's tongue. She'd heard it before, never again seeing a parent. Once they were home, relieved of their burden, they never set foot on her property again unless it was to drop off another child.

"And what about my other children? They certainly can't survive on breastmilk."

As if on cue, shadows began to move around the property.

Three outbuildings flanked the old house. Each one was dark, but the shapes that emerged from them were even darker. Into the headlights of the SUV walked Grammy's children—her Runts.

To her, they were perfect, but she knew how the rest of the world saw them. *Freaks.*

Janice's face morphed from grief to fear.

A large shadow appeared next to Grammy. She didn't have to turn to know it was Hammer. She knew he was armed, but hoped whatever weapon he carried wasn't obvious.

Shambling out of the darkness came more of her children.

While Grammy disapproved of the names the Runts gave each other as they were usually vile or downright mean, she knew it was part of their bonding and would never take that away. They were a family, like it or not.

Bull and Bags—the twins—were left at her front door without so much as a knock.

Grammy never found out who their parents were, and never asked; it didn't matter. Their parents had no fear of their discarded children trying to find their way home, thanks to the deformities cursed upon them.

Bull was, as he sounded, a bull of a boy, though he more closely resembled a cue ball than a bull. He was completely hairless and pale. But that wasn't what made his parents leave him. Bull was born without eyes, a nose, or ears. His eye sockets dimpled his face, but the skin was smooth. His nose was just two wet slits which acted as crude nostrils. Instead of ears, he had puckered holes on his head. They were only for show, as the large boy was also deaf.

Even as a kid, he was huge. Now that he was grown, he was even larger. He was shorter than Hammer, but wider. Even with the food being scarce, the layers of fat on him were endless.

His twin sister, Bags, was born without legs and only three fingers on each hand.

Apart, they were weak, but together, they were strong.

They moved into the light. Bags rode on her brother's back, attached by a crude harness. Her large, floppy breasts, which the others referred to as her 'saddlebags,' hung over the shoulders of her blind brother. A bit was in the blind boy's mouth, which his sister held onto.

Bull moved through the high snow like it was nothing, receiving his orders from the bit in his mouth.

Bags didn't say anything; she just watched with a sneer. Her three-fingered hands let the reins go slack, stopping her brother's movement. She traced something on the back of Bull's head, their way of communication, which she refused to teach anyone else.

The deaf and blind boy let out a deep laugh that was too loud. Drool ran down his smooth face, and he wiped it away with his hand.

Glump followed in Bull's wake, using the path created in the snow. He was squat, with arms that drug on the ground. He looked more like a chimp than a human, sans the hair. His neck was non-existent, and his knuckles were raw from the ground. Most of the Runts said he looked squished like a bug, but that wasn't how he'd gotten his name.

Even as a toddler, his parents knew something was wrong besides his physical deformities. When Glump would shit his diapers as a baby, he'd often blow them right out, creating a mess in the crib. It was when his mother received horrendous chemical burns after touching the feces that she realized something else was wrong.

As he aged, so did the ferocity of his stool. No matter what he ate, his shit became more and more powerful, melting whatever it would touch. After destroying his small bed as an infant, and the constant ridicule by the neighbors, his parents had enough, leaving him to the woods and Grammy's care.

Rocky walked out next. She was one of the older Runts, next to Hammer. The two of them were close, and Grammy feared they'd reproduce at some point, but even she didn't know if the young woman could handle the size of Hammer's cock. With one leg shorter than the other, she shambled with a crooked gait. Her limp wasn't the reason for her name, but her skin condition.

Brown patches of thick psoriasis sprouted all over her body, leaving her looking more like stone than human in some parts. She would've been average without the thick patch of brown scales running up the left side of her face and head, but she was bald where the scales grew, leaving her hair patchy.

More and more of them joined, but remained in the shadows, not wanting to be seen. Those were the youngest ones in the family, learning from their brothers and sisters. This was an important lesson for them, allowing them to see another story's beginning—another wayward soul, discarded by their blood relatives and left to their new family.

Grammy wanted to laugh at Janice's cries. Her children were special and unique, but she knew how they looked. It was good for Janice to see this and where she left her baby.

"As you can see, I have a lot of mouths to feed. What are you gonna do for them? For years, the people of Braxton brought us food and supplies, lessening my burden as I lessened theirs. What have you brought as an offering to help us?"

Beau left his wife cold and crying as he walked to the back of the SUV. He opened the hatch and grunted as he pulled something out.

A dead deer landed in the snow, puffing the fresh flakes into the air like a cloud of smoke. Blood ran from the gunshot wound in its chest.

A fresh kill.

"Here," he said, dragging the animal carcass next to his wife. "This is for you."

The Runts started to move, but Grammy raised her hand to stop them, knowing it wouldn't last long. They hadn't had fresh meat in a while, and she could hear the pitter-patter of drool hitting the snow as they salivated.

"Thank you, but please, bring more milk."

On cue, the baby in her arms cooed and began to writhe. The soft coos turned to cries as the wind blew.

Without another word, Grammy turned and began walking toward the house. She stopped next to Hammer. "Save a few chunks for me and the young'ins. Don't let them eat it all. And bring me the hide."

Hammer pulled a long knife from under his shirt; she knew he was armed. "Yes, Grammy."

Grammy smiled as she heard her children feeding and an engine revving as it sped away.

CHAPTER 9

The Sword was what Skylar expected—old tables, mismatched chairs, animal heads on the wall, and a jukebox that belched country music.

The four of them stood at the entrance, not knowing if they should seat themselves or not.

"Look at this place," Trenton whispered. "It's like we died and went to redneck heaven."

Skylar smirked, but he was right.

The parking lot was lined with lifted trucks and SUVs. Her brother's Toyota stuck out like a sore thumb, hidden between the American trucks. It was the only foreign vehicle in sight; the reliability of Japanese trucks hadn't made its way to Braxton yet.

A waitress, who looked in her forties but was probably closer to their age, wafted by carrying a tray of fried food. It didn't look the best, but it smelled terrific to the hungry teens.

"Sit wherever you'd like," she said. A cloud of cigarette smoke followed her, mingling with her cheap perfume and the scent of food. Her face was covered with makeup, and her uniform was so tight it did nothing to hide her pooch, undoubtedly left over from childbearing.

Skylar scanned the restaurant, which was busier than expected. She shouldn't have been surprised; it looked like the only place open in town.

A booth was open in the back corner but hadn't been bussed yet.

"Come on," she said, leading her little group toward the dirty table.

A crude catcall came from the bar as they walked past.

Men dressed in thick flannels and dirty hats enjoyed pitchers of beer and glasses of whiskey. They smoked and laughed, each of them eyeing her up and down.

Even though she was fully dressed in some of her thickest clothes, she still felt nude under their gaze.

"I bet that pussy is tighter than your sister's ass," one of the men said.

A wave of laughter and back pats erupted from the group.

"Probably has less hair too."

Another roar of drunken laughter and the sound of a fallen glass rushed from them.

Emmett slowed and turned.

"Don't," Skylar said, grabbing his arm. Her pulse raced, but she couldn't let him do anything stupid.

His tensed muscle was like corded metal under her fingers. A burst of unexpected lust ran through her as she remembered the night they had together. Her heart beat just a little faster.

After they'd had sex, Skylar was elated. Emmett had been the perfect lover, albeit she hadn't had many.

He was firm, yet gentle, allowing her to succumb to his will. It felt good to be treated right and cared for, something she didn't know was possible. Emmett took his time, ensuring she knew how much he desired her, and did his best to hold back his pleasure. When she'd come, she didn't think any other orgasm could hold a candle to it. She wasn't tense, allowing his body to pleasure hers.

After the waves of ecstasy abated and reality sank in, she began having regrets. It wasn't the sex she regretted, but the feelings.

There was just something about him. Ever since they'd been kids, there were little things she couldn't overlook. His appearance wasn't horrible, but her ex was damn near perfect when it came to looks. Emmett just didn't have *it*. There was nothing Skylar could put her finger on, but over the years, Emmett had been the butt of many jokes. Whether it was his ears, which were just a little too big, or his teeth, which were crooked despite the braces his parents spent thousands of dollars on, there was always something.

Skylar could see past the physical features, but didn't know if she could deal with the ridicule. It was a stupid reason to deny a good relationship, but deep down, she knew she couldn't handle the snide remarks. And sure, after college, who knew where they'd land? But there was just something about him that put people off. With her looks and brains, Skylar knew she could do better.

She felt like shit, like a shallow asshole, for even thinking that way, but she couldn't control her brain any more than Emmett could control his looks.

"Hell, I'm better looking than the pussy she's with," one of the drunkards yelled.

His buddies roared.

"None of us are as ugly as that kid. Even Grammy's kids look better than him. I heard one of 'em has a cock the size of a log."

"Bet that little slut has had all sorts of big dicks in her. Probably a few spooks, too," the originator said. He sucked down his drink but almost spit it up with laughter.

"If that's the case, count me out. I don't mess with that kinda girl."

"Patty, you don't mess with any type of girl, you ugly fuck," another of the group chimed in.

"Hey, fuck you." Patty's face turned red, his mousy features accented by the shame. "I fucked your sister, so that counts, right?"

The other men howled.

"Who hasn't fucked her?" the originator yelled. "Think half this bar, if not more, fucked Belinda. Even old Marty got his dick sucked by her. Ain't that right?"

A near-toothless old man, who looked like he'd never been sober, lifted his glass. "Best damn knobber I've ever had. And let me tell you, Old Marty's pole has been greased many times. Even by some of your grandmas."

Skylar and Emmett stood frozen from the backwoods banter.

"Told you, rednecks are nothing but big trucks and small dicks," Trenton said, appearing at their side. "Come on, let's sit down and see if we can salvage this night."

Skylar let go of Emmett's arm. She knew her friend was right. They were hundreds of miles from home, stuck in a blizzard, and starving. Picking a fight with a bunch of assholes would do none of them any good. She didn't want to see her friends get hurt.

Skylar pulled Emmett's arm, breaking his gaze from the drunks.

They'd moved on to talking about other bullshit, leaving them alone.

"Buy me a drink?" Skylar asked.

The softness of her voice, an almost seductive request, broke Emmett's glare. He turned to her with fury in his eyes. It was a part of him she didn't often see, and it made her tingle.

"Yeah, sure. Hopefully, we don't get asked for ID."

They looked around at the mass of people. "I highly doubt they'll care about a beer or two." Skylar snaked her arm under his.

Emmett pulled her in tightly and smiled with his crooked teeth. "You're probably right. Let's see if this place has anything decent to eat."

CHAPTER 10

The warm blood of the deer steamed in the cold night. Fresh snow turned red around the carcass as raw meat was consumed by misshapen mouths.

Hammer sliced a chunk of meat from the hind quarter of the deer and tucked it into the pocket of his overalls. Grammy hadn't been eating much lately, and he knew the warm, bloody slice would be enough for her. She would have to boil it for a while to eat it; her teeth weren't the best and she'd lost a few over the last few months.

The smell of offal was strong as some of the Runts ate the entrails.

"Dis is pretty good," said Glump. His face was smeared with the green stain of the deer's stomach matter. The stench would repulse most people, but not the Runts.

"We haven't had fresh meat in so long, I almost forgot how good it was," Bags said. She was in the snow, ripping chunks from the carcass.

Next to her, Bull waited for a piece of flesh to be

put into his hand. His eyeless face stared into the darkness of the night.

"Here," Bags said, handing a piece to her brother.

Bull took it and smiled, cramming the meat into his mouth. Blood ran down his chin as he ate.

"Yeah, it's been a while," said Froggy. His bulging eyes and webbed fingers made naming easy for the other Runts. "Not since Pickles died."

Pickles was one of the oldest Runts. His skin was bumpy, full of blisters and sores. His skin had a green hue, and he always had a slight stench of vinegar.

When Grammy found him dead one morning, she wept, but she knew he couldn't go to waste. Food wasn't something they came across often, especially meat. It had taken a while to convince her, but she didn't resist much.

Pickles's body was butchered with crude efficiency and shared. Thanks to his mutation, most of his skin was bad, but the flesh underneath was perfect. Some of it was preserved and dried, but most was eaten raw by his hungry siblings.

"Ah, Pickles," Bags said. Her hands were red with gore. "He was a good one." She stuffed a piece of venison into her mouth.

Pickles had been a good one—*too* good. He wasn't the first person they'd eaten, thanks to Grammy, but he was the first one they *knew* they'd eaten. At first, they were all skeptical of his meat. He was one of them, a mutant, but starvation was a real threat, and his meat kept them going.

When he was cooked up with some old onions and spices, the Runts went wild. His meat was some of the best they'd had, and since that day, they all craved it. It was something that always lurked in the backs of their minds. Each of them looked at the other like a potential meal, wondering who would die next. It was macabre and sick, but they couldn't help it.

Hammer loved venison, but the taste of humans beat everything else. He often wondered what baby tasted like. He'd heard of veal, tender, baby cows that were milk-fed and slaughtered before they became too old.

When he was young, the people of Braxton would bring them food. It wasn't much, a few cans here and there or the occasional poor cut of meat that smelled slightly off, but it had been something. Now, things have changed. Grammy supplied them with what she could, but sometimes, it wasn't enough.

They hunted, at least the ones that could make their way through the woods without making a racket, but squirrels and woodchucks would only get you so far.

The townsfolk hated them, yet knew Grammy was a savior. Few of them had the guts to kill their kin, so they'd drop them with her. It was just more mouths to feed, and the food was scarce at best.

Hammer needed meat, and a lot of it. He was massive and not only south of his belt line. Even with his deformities, God granted him something special. His frame was wide, bigger than any man he'd seen. Thick muscles covered his body, and he knew he'd be even bigger with more food. Swinging the axe to split wood felt like nothing, even when some of his siblings would be left gasping for air. He could do it all day and night, if possible. The axe felt like a toothpick in his hands. And when the sun went down, his calloused hands focused elsewhere.

He didn't realize he had a monster cock until he

saw the others naked. It was the size of an arm and just as thick. When he'd stroke himself, he needed two hands for it to feel good enough to shoot his spunk. One time, he tried to put it in Bags's hairy pussy, but she screamed and hollered. Hammer had to settle for sliding it between her sagging tits and blasting a load of his baby batter on her ugly face. He didn't think he'd ever get the chance to fuck willingly, and he wouldn't hurt his sister with his cock.

"What about the baby?" Bags asked. She rubbed her hands in the snow. Her nipples were hard, and her tits rested on her stomach. "Not much meat, but I bet she's tender."

"Yeah, imagine the stew Grammy could make with that one," Glump said. He wiped his mouth with the back of his hand. His rheumy eyes shone with hope. "Maybe she has a jar of beets in the cellar. Oh boy, that'd be the best ever."

"I couldn't imagine the horrific shit you'd take after eating beets," Froggy said. He squatted low, posing like his namesake.

"It doesn't matter what he eats, Glump still has to shit outside," Hammer said. "No fucking exceptions." He drew his knife and pointed it at the other mutant. It was meant as a joke, but the fear on Glump's face was real.

"I-I know that, Hammer," Glump sputtered. Shame painted his face.

Hammer put a massive, deformed hand on his shoulder. "I'm just fucking with ya."

Glump smiled, his teeth stained red. He still looked scared, but slightly less so. "Yeah, yeah, I know." He looked back at the mutilated carcass but didn't grab another piece.

"Bags has a point. That fucking baby is just another mouth to feed. And what she eats comes right from our bellies."

The rest of them stopped eating and looked at him. Deformed faces, red with blood, stared at him in the light of the moon.

"That screaming thing probably won't make it through the winter, but she can keep us full for a few days with her tender meat."

"There's a whole town of meat down the mountain," Froggy said. "We should go snatch one of them fuckers. They think we're monsters anyway. Why not live up to it?"

Hammer had considered it before. It wouldn't be hard to hide in the woods and grab a hunter or two during the fall. The sheriff would come looking, that was a fact, but the evidence would be gone and eaten, turned into shit by then.

Grammy would never let them.

The townsfolk wouldn't stand for it. If enough of them wanted to, they'd kill all the Runts. They didn't have guns or cars, at least ones running.

Hammer was strong and could swing an axe, but against a firearm, he was outmatched.

"That would be great until a whole lot of them showed up with guns and shit," Bags said as she fed Bull another piece of deer meat.

Hammer wiped his hands on his stained overalls. Bags was right, but Froggy was too. There was a whole town of food below them. If the people of Braxton wouldn't feed them, they needed to take what was theirs. He touched the chunk of meat in his pocket. A cold wind blew, moving the few strands of greasy hair he had left on his misshapen head.

Grammy stood in the window. The dim light from the lantern glowed behind her as she rocked the baby.

Hammer trudged through the snow, following his massive footprints.

The house wasn't warm, but it was better than being outside. He didn't realize how his hunger overwhelmed his sense of temperature until he was back inside.

"Did you get enough?" Grammy asked. She smiled down at the cooing baby.

Hammer pulled a chair from the crooked table and sat. He took the piece of meat from his overalls and set it down. Cool blood ran from it, staining the wood. "No, we never have enough. You know that."

Pulling a bottle of milk from a pot on the fire, Grammy touched it to her arm, testing the temperature. It must've been good because she stuck the nipple in the baby's mouth. "Maybe you and your siblings should go out on a hunt tomorrow. See if you can bring down another deer or a few squirrels." She rocked the baby as it fed.

"No, that's not enough. We might be able to scrounge more meat from the deer, but it will only last for so long," Hammer said, licking his crusty lips.

Grammy ignored him and focused on the nursing infant.

"What about her?" Hammer asked. Initially, he didn't realize it, but he'd drawn his knife. "She may not be big, but there's meat on her bones. Won't be enough to get us through the winter, but will keep some of us fed, at least."

Pulling the baby closer to her withered breasts, Grammy said, "I will not have talk like that in this house. She's your sister now. And God forbid she dies, no one will touch her. Understood?"

Hammer stared at her. He loved her and trusted her, but she was wrong. A baby had no part in their family. There were enough mouths to feed without adding another. When he was younger, it was different. The people of Braxton respected them, bringing food and supplies. That had changed. Some might not make it through the winter, and they both knew that. Grammy was putting the baby before them, and that didn't sit right with him. "Fine, but we need to hunt. We need to do something. Animals are too hard to kill, especially without a gun. But people…" he let his thought die on the tip of his tongue.

Grammy brushed the wispy hair from the baby's face. She smiled as the baby fed, sucking down the milk. She was silent, tending to the baby, who, at the time, had no name.

"We're just asking you permission to go hunt. That's all."

Grammy smiled at the baby, who was growing fussy after the last of the breast milk was finished. "Don't go into town. We can't have that. They'll come for us if you do that. As it is, every missing person gets blamed on us. I have to scrape and beg, proving our innocence when we've done nothing wrong."

Hammer nodded. "No, we won't go into town, but let us hunt the roads. We have passersby that come through. They're travelers, easy pickins if you ask me. People go missing in these mountains. It's just a fact of nature. And now, with the storm, it's even better. One car off the roadway can keep us in meat for a while. Grammy, we might not make it without."

Grammy put the fussy baby over her shoulder and patted her on the back. She shushed her, but to no avail.

She looked at her oldest son, the one who'd been with her the longest, the one she loved more than anything. "Go, but be discrete about it. Leave no survivors. For the good of our family, you and your siblings may hunt. But no locals, only travelers."

Smiling, further distorting his already mutated face, Hammer reached down and touched his knife. The cold steel felt warm in his lumpy fingers. A rush of blood filled his brain with the thought of human meat. The blood rushed not only to his brain, but to the appendage he was named after. He grabbed an old coat from the rack as he headed back outside.

He walked over to one of the outbuildings and grabbed a rusty pickaxe.

The rest of the Runts watched as he walked toward their little group.

"Dress warm, Runts. Tonight, we hunt."

A group of bloody, smiling mutated faces looked at him, breaking their concentration on the bare deer carcass. As one, they cheered, screaming a horrifying shriek into the night sky.

CHAPTER 11

The Volvo SUV carved through the snow. All four wheels were equipped with fresh rubber, and the luxury car was made for the heavy snow. The all-wheel-drive system was one of the best in the world, which was a big selling point for Chip and Karen Sellmers.

The car had been a present for Karen, but Chip used it more. He commuted much further than his wife, and her BMW 3 Series was just fine. When they bought the car, Chip told his wife he'd take the Beemer and leave her with the Volvo, but when Karen had woken up on the first day of ownership, her husband had taken the new car. Since then, and after many fights, Karen succumbed to the will of her husband, something she never thought possible. But after twenty years of marriage, it was commonplace.

"Can you believe they went for that deal?" Chip asked. He was driving faster than he should've been, especially after one martini too many.

The snow whipped past them in a blur, making it look like they were in space.

"I mean, that lot should've sold for at least 900k. We pretty much stole it for 500."

Karen was reapplying lipstick in the visor mirror. Even though they were on their way back to the hotel and wouldn't arrive for a few hours, she still felt the need to freshen up. She knew her husband would want his dick sucked, at least to get him hard. Then, it would be a minute of sex, tops, before his semi-erect cock unleashed a pathetic load into her. It was a familiar routine in their marriage, but it was their life, the life they'd made together over the years.

Chip liked seeing his flaccid cock in his wife's mouth when her lips were red. There were a few nights, especially when they were younger and struggling, when the red came from her blood. Chip wasn't as free with his fists as he used to be, but if he couldn't get hard or lost his erection partway through the brief fuck, he'd get mad.

When Karen put a gun to his head, a la Karen Hill in *Goodfellas*, the beatings lessened, but part of Karen missed them. No, she wasn't crazy, but something about her husband showing passion for something other than money or screwing someone over did something to her.

The few friends she had called her nuts to let a man not only put his hands on her, but then to let him fuck her afterward. But there was something about it that made her wet. Even far into her fifties, Karen still felt the slickness of lust, though her orgasms came via the various sex toys she had in her nightstand.

Karen blew a kiss at the mirror, ignoring the creases around her lips, before slamming the visor shut. "It was a great deal, hun." She rubbed his thigh. "And I know what you like after a good deal." Even without her mouth on him, Karen felt her husband's cock begin to stiffen.

Chip looked over at her with a grin. "I haven't seen you this happy since you got Marta deported. Fucking spic bitch thinking she could steal from us? Not on our watch, that's for damn sure."

The maid was the first suspect when Karen's tennis bracelet went missing. Karen was furious and looking for blood. She had no idea her husband had taken it and given it to one of his aides as payment for a rough bout of anal. He wasn't particularly well endowed, but a no-prep ass fuck could have horrible consequences. Rather than deal with the fallout of sexual misconduct, Chip made it up to the girl in the only way he knew how—money.

"I loved that bracelet. Besides, I was getting sick of Marta anyway. It was time for her to go."

"The look on her face when ICE showed up was priceless. I hope she's happy in whatever shithole she was sent back to." Chip didn't hate the housekeeper as much as his wife did. Oftentimes, he'd fuck her when Karen was stuck late at work. He even paid for two abortions during her stay with them. He couldn't have a bastard running around like Schwarzenegger.

"I think it was Guatemala, but I could be wrong," Karen said, still kneading her husband's cock through his Kenneth Cole pants. He was growing harder under her touch.

"It doesn't matter. It was a shithole country. Hell, anywhere in South America is way worse than here." Chip leaned back slightly, allowing his wife to stroke him better.

"Ain't that the truth. You know, we should think about buying up some property down there. I heard

Costa Rica is a great investment."

Chip nodded, taking another turn too fast.

The car slid in the rising snow but held the road.

"That's a great idea, babe. I'm still flying high on getting that lot. Dumb fucks thought we'd back out of the deal so the hospital could buy it cheap and make it into a burn ward." He chuckled and groaned as he became fully erect. "Dumb fucks never dealt with the Sellmers before."

Some buyers were cutthroat regarding real estate, but Chip and Karen were a different breed altogether. They'd screw anyone over if it meant a better price. Lie, beg, cheat, and steal, it was all fair game.

"Why don't you whip that cock out and let me start on you right now?"

Chip looked over at his wife. His capped teeth shone bright in the light of the gauges. Even his horseshoe bald spot reflected the soft light. "Baby, you read my mind. I'll take care of you when we get home. Just let me get this nut out now."

Karen knew that was a lie. Her husband hadn't made her cum in a decade or more, and even that was her own doing. When he could hold his load long enough, she'd ride him. She had to grind on his pelvis because too much up and down motion would make him bust immediately.

"Deal," she said, knowing it was bullshit. But she also couldn't work him up like she'd done without doing something. A hand job was out of the question. He wouldn't bust on his pants, and she wasn't in the mood to fuck in the car. Besides, she didn't want his cum leaking out of her for the next couple of hours.

Chip pushed his seat back enough to still reach the gas pedal as Karen unzipped his fly.

She worked his cock free from his designer pants, getting a whiff of his sweaty crotch.

He groaned as she took him into her warm mouth.

CHAPTER 12

Bull couldn't see for shit, but Bags knew how to control her blind brother. Without sound or sight, Bags guided the big oaf to the fallen log. With the help of Hammer, the two of them (well, three, technically) dragged the dead tree into the road. It wasn't huge, but more than enough to slow anyone unlucky enough to be out in the storm.

Steam rose from Hammer's scalp as fat snowflakes melted on his misshapen head. He was sweaty from moving the log but felt good. It felt promising. Their plan was simple, and it had to work.

The log wasn't there to destroy a car, but to get them to stop. If the vehicle looked like it belonged in Braxton, a truck, or lifted SUV, they'd let the occupants move the log and carry on. If they were out of towners, the Runts would attack once they stopped. It was simple, yet would be effective.

In the shadows of the trees, the Runts hid and waited. Snow fell heavily and silent, creating a blanket of white.

"How fucking long are we waiting?" Froggy asked. His big eyes reflected the gray light of the night sky. He blew into his webbed fingers before jamming them under his arms. His coat was threadbare and old. It didn't have nearly the warmth of Hammer's, but Froggy wasn't as important, and he knew that.

"As long as we have to," Hammer said, leaning the pickaxe against a nearby tree. He sat on a downed log that was far too big for them to move.

"Not too much longer," Bags said from the back of her brother, Bull. "I'm freezing my tits off."

Hammer smiled. "I doubt those floppers would freeze off. Besides, they're keeping Bull's shoulders warm. Ain't that right?" he asked, knowing the big boy couldn't see or hear. "Eh, he knows what I'm saying, even if he can't hear."

The human horse called Bull shivered. His white scalp was wet with melting snow running down his face like tears.

"Yeah, Hammer. I'm gonna have to shit soon. That deer meat did a number on my guts," Glump said. He clutched his stomach and winced in pain.

"Good, go take a shit over there," Hammer pointed. "And bring back that steaming pile. We might be able to use it."

"My shit? Why in the fuck would you want that?"

"Your shit is rank and nasty, but it has its purposes. You ever see anything melt something like your shit does? Hell no, and neither have I. It's repulsive, just like you, but it has a purpose."

"Just like me?"

Hammer shrugged. "Yeah, sure."

Bright-white headlights reflected off the snow. A new SUV, definitely not belonging to anyone in

Braxton, cut through the storm.

"Look alive, everyone. Here comes dinner," Hammer said.

"And breakfast and lunch," Bags said, riding Bull next to the big mutant.

A stench permeated the air as Glump came running back. He carried a flat rock covered in human shit. The feces bubbled and popped like hot tar. "What'd I miss?"

"Shh," Hammer said, putting a finger to his deformed lips. "Fresh meat." His nose wrinkled. "Have that nasty shit ready to go."

"What do you want me to do with it?"

"I don't know, but you'll figure it out."

Glump smiled and nodded, holding the shit-covered rock like a prized possession.

Hammer grabbed the pickaxe, wringing the weathered wood in his firm grasp. He smiled, letting the soft light of the hidden moon reflect off his mangled teeth.

***

"Fuck," Chip groaned as he came. He pushed down on the back of Karen's head, jamming his cock as far down her throat as it would go.

She gagged, but that only turned him on more.

He felt himself softening as the orgasm ebbed away with every spurt of his cock snot. Finally, after he was spent, he let go of his wife's head.

Karen sprung up like a jack-in-the-box and swallowed his sour spunk with a grimace. Her lipstick was smeared on her cheeks like a low-budget Joker and her mascara ran, leaving her face looking like a raccoon.

Chip tucked his wet penis away, doing his best to keep the car on the road as he did.

A small pearl of cum wet his underwear, but at the moment, he didn't care. His post-orgasm bliss removed any sense of discomfort, at least for the time being.

"Damn, babe. You still have it. Even after all these years, you still know your way around a blow job."

Karen grunted her approval as she did what she could to make herself look decent. She took a makeup wipe from her purse and wiped at her eyes and face, doing her best to clear up the mess.

"Oh, what the actual fuck?" Chip groaned as he slowed the car.

A tree lay in the road, blocking their path.

"This is just great. I go from having a perfect night to a shit one in a matter of seconds."

Karen shut the visor, not happy with the final result of her cleanup, but it was the best she could do. "I think I saw a road a ways back."

Chip waved her off. "Ah, what the fuck do you know? You were face down in my crotch, remember?"

Karen swallowed hard, letting him know she sure as shit still remembered.

"I'll have to turn back or try to get by it."

"Don't go around it, Chip. If we get stuck, we'll be fucked."

He didn't want to admit it, but his wife was right. Getting stuck in the snow would be worse than a long detour.

"Fuck me." Chip pulled over as far as he dared and cut the wheel. He'd have to do a K-turn and go back the way they'd come.

The car crawled through the high snow as he nosed

it closer to the woods on the opposite side of the road.

Chip focused on the front of the vehicle, not bothering to look into the treeline.

Karen screamed, and he almost backhanded her out of instinct.

"What the fuck?" he yelled, looking at his hysterical wife.

She pointed at the woods.

Something was coming toward them.

Something big.

Something fast and holding a pickaxe.

***

Hammer didn't wait for the rest of them. The car was in the perfect position. He rushed forward, slipping as he did, holding his pickaxe tight in his grasp. His old boots struggled to find traction, but his will to kill and feed propelled him forward.

He slammed the axe through the car's hood and into the engine block with a mighty swing. A shock reverberated through his arms, shaking his bones.

Metal screamed as he tried to free it, but it held fast, stuck in the dying motor. Smoke poured from the hole he created, and a sickly-sweet fluid ran onto the snow-covered ground.

Two people—a male and a female—were locked in a scream.

They screamed, and Hammer laughed as the rest of the Runts poured out of the trees.

Rounding the car, Hammer grabbed the driver's door and yanked on the handle, hoping it would be that easy. The handle resisted, and he snapped it clean off the vehicle in his fury.

The man behind the wheel screamed and climbed away from Hammer. He trampled over the woman next to him, nearly jumping into her lap as he did.

Hammer took a long knife from his belt and tapped on the window. He smiled at the couple inside, letting drool run from his vile mouth. With his deformed hand, he punched the glass.

The window held, sending a shock wave up his arm. His knuckles split, weeping blood. This only enraged him further. He struck again, but the glass still held.

A smear of his gore marked the window, eliciting more screams from the frightened passengers.

Froggy jumped on the hood of the car, avoiding the protruding pickaxe. He kicked at the windshield, cracking it, but not getting through. Again, he kicked, but the glass held as if it had a layer of plastic in it. "Fucking bitch!" Another kick sent even more fractures through the weakening glass.

Bags, Bull, and Glump trudged to the passenger side through the snow.

The terrified occupants did their best to move away from them, but they were surrounded.

Bags pulled on Bull's reigns, signaling him to crouch. She was at eye level with the couple, looking through the window. The look of sheer disgust on the woman's face when she saw the deformities Bags had been cursed with only enraged the Runt even more.

"Hey, cunt," Bags said. "I'm gonna shove this," she pulled a hammer from behind her back, "up your stinking pussy." Her three fingers wrapped clumsily around the wooden grip. She wound up and swung, shattering the glass.

Hammer stopped punching at the sound of glass

breaking.

Screams, which were once held back by the window, ripped through the air.

He whooped and hollered, abandoning his assault on the window, and ran around to the passenger side, sensing a kill. And more than a kill, but meat.

"Fuck you!" the woman screamed.

She was dressed much nicer than anyone the Runts had ever seen. Her dress glittered in the light of the moon, as did her jewelry.

Bags stared at the woman's small breasts, which were pushed up to the top of her dress. Envy and hatred puckered her face with disgust. She could only think of the droopy sacks of flesh that hung down her brother's shoulders and chest. Well, by the end of the night, she'd have a new set of tits, that was certain.

The Runts rushed to the vehicle's passenger side, ripping at the woman.

The man pushed her toward them as he moved back to the driver's seat in a frenzy.

"Help me!" she screamed, but the man was no help. Broken glass glittered on her lap, blending with the shininess of her dress. She fought and punched as mutated hands tore at her clothes. The woman moved from the Runts and put her feet up, kicking with the sharp heels of her shoes.

Hammer felt his monster cock swelling as the hem of the terrified woman's dress rose, exposing her underwear. They were wet with her fear piss, and he could smell it coming off her in waves. The outline of her sex was easily visible, and the wet fabric clung to her.

She kicked and thrashed, cutting herself on the bits of broken glass.

The prospect of a meal went to the back of Hammer's mind and something else took the front. Something he'd never had, but that would finally come to an end.

"Chip, for fuck's sake, help me!" The terrified woman screamed, but no one answered.

The driver's door flung open, and the man took off running. He was dressed as fancy as the woman, and Hammer knew he wouldn't get far, not wearing slick, black shoes.

"Glump, get his ass," Hammer ordered without taking his eyes off his prize in the car. He reached into the vehicle and took a heel to the face. The lump of his mutated flesh split, oozing blood and pus down his cheek. "Bitch. You have no idea how bad I'm gonna hurt you." He held the knife up for effect, but that wasn't the tool he planned on using.

The warmth of his cock was unbearable as it ran down his leg. It seemed to have a mind of its own, wanting to rise, but held down by old denim.

***

Glump enjoyed the peep show he was getting. He'd never seen pussy before, except for the mangled hole between Bags's stumps. That was the only one he'd seen, and if they all looked as hairy and gross as hers, he didn't think he'd ever want to stick his cock in one. But when the fancy lady started kicking, he'd caught a glimpse of her wet outline, and boy, oh boy did it look good. Even soaked in piss and hidden behind her underwear, he knew it was nice. He couldn't wait for Hammer to yank her out of the car so that he could rip those piss-soaked undies off her.

"Glump, get his ass," Hammer yelled.

Glump heard his name but was confused for a second. His tiny pecker was hard and wet, and for some reason, the massive mutant was yelling at him. *Whose ass am I getting? I'd much rather have her ass.* And then, he saw the man running from the car. "Oh fuck." Glump took off, nearly losing his footing in the snow. He still carried the rock full of his corrosive shit in his hand. The nasty shit wouldn't hurt him, his flesh was the only thing it didn't seem to damage, but it smelled like Hell. Even if it didn't hurt him, he still didn't want to be covered in it.

The rock wasn't big, but Glump wasn't very fast. Hammer should've sent Froggy after the man, but the bug-eyed mutant was nowhere to be found.

"Fucker," Glump grunted, debating on dropping the stone in the snow.

The man slipped. His black shoes were too smooth, and his pace too frantic. He landed hard on his face in the tree line, kicking up a cloud of fresh powder.

Glump was closing on him as the man rose to his feet.

Froggy emerged from the darkness and swung a thick branch, catching the man in the face as he scrambled up.

Perfect white teeth flew from the man's mouth, carrying with them spurts of gore. They left holes of red in the snow as they landed.

"Thought you were gonna get away that easy, huh?" Froggy asked. He wound up and swung again, catching the man in the back of the skull.

The branch shattered into pieces, flying into the snow.

The man, dazed and injured, did something neither

of them expected—he attacked. He rushed Froggy on all fours, taking the Runt in the stomach.

Froggy's eyes bulged even further, which Glump didn't think possible. His brother went down in a heap, with the man on top of him in a flurry of snow and fists.

Both of them grunted as the fight ramped up. Froggy's webbed hands balled into fists as he did his best to fight off the bigger man, but without a weapon, he was fucked.

Glump ran up to them, sinking in the deep snow. He scooped the pile of his rancid shit in his hands and discarded the rock, which sizzled as it hit the snow.

Without another second of hesitation, he jumped on the man's back and wrapped one arm around his neck. When he had some control of the man's head, he struck. Glump smeared his vile excrement into the man's bloody mouth and face. The stench of shit and melting flesh was heavy in the winter air.

A bloodcurdling scream erupted from the man's melting mouth.

Red and brown chunks of bloody shit fell onto the snow, hissing as they landed.

Glump mushed chunks of poorly digested feces up the man's nose. He dropped the man as Froggy wriggled his way out from underneath him.

Froggy was bleeding from the attack, but he smiled as the destruction of the man's face had just begun.

The flesh on the lower portion of his face was gone. White bone mixed with pink and brown blended with the remaining muscle and skin. His tongue was blistered and dripping like candle wax as the putrid slurry ate its way through the meat. The gaps in his gumline left from his missing teeth burned away as globs of acidic shit found their way in. His mouth crackled as it dissolved.

Warm goo ran down his ruined face as his eyes melted away. The delicate orbs burst like overripened blueberries. But instead of sweet juice, ocular fluid, shit, and blood poured forth.

Froggy laughed—no, croaked—at the sight before him.

The man clawed blindly at his face, only furthering his agony as his fingers scraped away more destroyed flesh.

Hellish shit ate through the tips of his fingers when they touched the lumps.

Drawing an old screwdriver from his belt, Glump went to work. The gurgling moans were replaced with the wet sucking sounds of stabbing as he plunged the tool into the man's back. Metal gouged bone, digging into the meat, seeking organs. Again and again, he stabbed. Each thrust turned the black fabric of the fancy jacket wetter and wetter with rich blood.

The snow around them drank the gore with each thrust.

Glump felt the warmth on his fist, giving him some reprieve from the cold snow. His mutated face was locked in a rictus grin of pleasure and fury.

The man stopped moving, but Glump didn't stop his assault. Each stab was a statement, a hate-mail letter to the world that had discarded them. It was something he'd never felt before. All the love Grammy showed them was nothing compared to the world's hatred. The perfection of others, the love, it was a life he envied and loathed in one.

A hand with webbed fingers grabbed his arm, stopping the assault. "I think he's dead."

Glump panted. The blood on his skin and clothing was cooling as the snow continued to fall around him.

"We don't want to fuck the meat up any more than we have to," Froggy said. His face was swelling, which didn't help his already freakish appearance. "Come on, let's go help the others with this one's bitch." He darted off into the snow toward the Volvo.

Glump stabbed the cooling corpse one last time and followed his brother.

The night was far from over.

***

Hammer had to give it to the woman; she was putting up a hell of a fight. He saw Froggy and Glump rushing back to him. Froggy's face was bruised and bleeding, but he noticed the gore coating Glump's clothes and hands. The screwdriver was red and had bits of meat and fabric stuck to it. Hammer chuckled.

"Your man is fucking dead, bitch. But he got off easy. No, I'm gonna have fun with you. I'm gonna fuck you and eat you. And then, maybe, I'll let you die."

Another kick darted at his face from the car's interior, but he was ready for it. With his lumpy, strong hand, he grasped her ankle. He planted his feet as best as he could and yanked.

The woman screamed as her knee tore and hip dislocated.

Hammer pulled again, ripping her from the car onto the snowy road.

Still, she fought even though the pain of her injury must've been immense.

He grabbed at the woman, snagging the top of her dress.

The glittery fabric tore, exposing her tits. Her nipples were dark against the creamy-white flesh of her breasts, which looked much too round and firm.

After seeing Bags and Grammy's chests, Hammer expected something different. The swelling of his cock reached painful proportions, and he needed to release it for fear of it bursting in his pants.

Bare-breasted, cold, and injured, the woman still fought. Her painted nails dug into Hammer's mutated flesh, leaving rents of pus and blood.

Bags pulled on Bull's reins, trying to get the large mutant into the fight. She had control over him, but they'd never been in such a situation.

The blind, deaf, and dumb mutant shuffled forward, doing his best to follow the commands of his legless rider.

With one damaged leg, the woman used her good one to maneuver herself. She scrambled, trying to find purchase on the slick asphalt under the snow.

Again, Bags pulled the reins, yanking her brother's lips and mouth as she did.

The big mutant awkwardly danced, narrowly avoiding falling on the woman. His big body shuddered, and he let out a deep moan from his misshapen mouth.

Looking down, to Bags's shock and fear, the bitch was biting her brother. Her clean, white teeth ripped through the fetid clothing around Bull's ankle.

Bull shook and shuddered in pain.

Bags did everything she could to control him and stay in her harness.

Reacting out of instinct and pain, Bull lifted his foot and stomped. His rotten boot hit the woman in the face, driving her skull into the snowy road.

Her nose crunched and shattered. The back of her skull deformed, cracking like a watermelon. Brain matter and blood stained the snow around her like the halo of a fallen angel. Her eyes, which were dark with makeup, looked up dead. A flurry of snowflakes landed on the lifeless orbs, melting with the remaining bits of body heat.

"You dumb fuck!" Hammer wailed. He punched Bull in the face, splitting the skin on his cheek with his already bloody fist.

Bull staggered and spun in fear, trying to avoid another strike.

"Hey, what the fuck?" Bags said. She tightened her grip on the reins with her three-fingered hand. Once Bull was steady, she released her grip and rubbed her brother's face. She kissed his bald head with her crooked lips, doing her best to quell the massive beast.

"Your fucking idiot brother killed her. She was mine!" Hammer held his knife in his hand, showing it to Bags.

Glump and Froggy cowered, not wanting to draw any of Hammer's ire.

"I was gonna finally get some pussy. God knows your nasty slit couldn't handle the hammer. And I'm sick and tired of fucking your saddle bags."

Froggy moved in, crouching low near the dead woman. He rubbed her bare breasts with his webbed hands, pinching her nipples hard. "She's still warm, Hammer. You could still do what you need to do. But—but can I go first?" He was rubbing his erection through his pants.

"Yeah, give us a run before you ruin her," Glump interjected with bravery fueled by horniness and Froggy's confidence.

"Fuck you. The lot of you. You can have her when I'm done." Hammer began undoing his crusty overalls. "Now, each of you grab a leg and help me pick her up."

They did as they were told, grunting under the exertion of the dead weight. Together, they brought her corpse to the front of the vehicle.

Hammer lifted her torso as high as he could and slammed her down onto the pickax jutting from the ruined hood.

The spike punched through her ribs, shooting out between her breasts. Heart blood ran warm and red, wetting her dress.

"Take an ankle and spread her wide." Hammer dropped his overalls to the snowy ground.

His cock was horrifying. It was nearly two feet long and thick as a man's thigh. His foreskin was taut, exposing his wet glans. The purple head was as thick as a grapefruit, with a piss slit that could pass a golf ball.

Glump and Froggy spread the corpse's legs, exposing her underwear.

Hammer ripped the dainty fabric away, revealing the dead vagina.

Snowflakes landed on the trimmed pubic hair, glistening like morning dew.

Hammer hocked back and spat a thick wad of spit into his lumpy palm. He greased up his swollen shaft and positioned himself in front of the corpse. The massive tip of his dick pressed against her narrow opening, spreading her dead lips. He pushed, forcing himself into the corpse.

Flesh tore and blood ran as he made the opening wider. The narrow strip of skin separating the corpse's asshole and pussy ripped, creating one shit-and-blood-filled cavern. Hammer pushed further, feeling the dead flesh tear.

"Pull harder," he instructed. Snow melted on his deformed face, running down the canyons of misshapen skin.

Glump and Froggy pulled as he fucked. With each bit of pressure they applied, more of the corpse ripped.

Hammer pushed deeper, burying half his cock into the body. The warmth and wetness were almost too much for him, but he held out. "More," he ordered.

The other Runts pulled, tearing more of the flesh.

Ramming further, Hammer pushed past the resistance of innards.

The corpse's stomach bulged as his massive member made its way beyond her reproductive parts and into her gut.

He felt like he was fucking a bag of slimy snakes as the tip of his dick forced its way into her intestines. Shit and partially processed food coated his veiny shaft as he began to fuck with purpose.

"Pull this bitch apart!" He fucked the corpse like a man possessed.

Melted snow mixed with sweat as he fucked and fucked. A seam of torn flesh opened her belly, exposing smooth muscle.

His member rippled through the hole like a groundhog under the earth as he thrusted faster. The squelching of his assault on the corpse was loud and stunk like old roadkill. With one final balls-deep thrust, he shuddered and came.

Cum, shit, blood, and stomach matter rushed from the gory cavern as he pulled his cock from the corpse. She was nearly split in half.

Hammer's wilting cock was grotesque, coated in

all matters of filth. His foreskin was slowly covering the leaking mushroom of his dick head.

Globs of leftover cum landed in the snow as he grabbed his cock and gave it a shake before stuffing it back into his pants.

Then, Hammer put his soiled hand to his misshapen nose and sniffed. "Ah, now that was some good pussy. I could use that more often." He looked at Froggy and Glump who were still strangely erect. "She's all yours, boys. When you're done, bring the meat back to the house. Grammy is gonna make us a good supper tonight." The big mutant walked into the dark snowfall.

There was nothing left for his brothers to fuck, at least not in the corpse's pussy, but they were resourceful and horny.

He laughed when he heard the sounds of wet fucking and grunting.

CHAPTER 13

Trent wished Emmett and Skylar would stop playing games and fuck again. And make it real, not some drunken hookup.

He and Skylar had always been close. She didn't have many girlfriends growing up, and he knew he was gay from an early age. Trenton was not interested in the boy *activities*, only the boys themselves. So, when the girls needed help with fashion or had boy troubles, he was always there for them, and they were there for him, especially Skylar. Like the others, he was thrilled when they all settled on the same school.

Even in 2025, it was tough being gay. Sure, there were plenty of movements and laws that helped fight the struggle, but more than a few assholes still existed. He would've found allies and like-minded people on a college campus, but it was better to roll in with a group of friends. Besides, he and Skylar talked all the time and about everything.

When she decided to try anal for the first time, Trent gave her a whole lesson on cleanout, lube, and the pleasure associated with it. Of course, they had different internal parts, but he knew what kind of nut he busted from a good ass fuck.

The night after Skylar and Emmett had sex, Trent was elated, but they were two of his closest friends, and he knew Jackson would approve. Not that Skylar needed her brother's approval, but it helped ease the tension.

Jackson didn't care for Skylar's ex, Derek, but the thought of his friend fucking his sister wasn't the best thought to have.

Trent knew Jackson approved of Emmett, even if he didn't want to hear all the details.

When Skylar came to Trent's room crying, he knew something was wrong. She moaned and cried about it being a mistake, that she couldn't have a life with Emmett. After a little weed and a long talk, Trent questioned her. Emmett was the perfect guy: smart, caring, funny, and, according to Skylar, a great lay. But at the end of the talk, Skylar spilled her guts.

She didn't find Emmett wholly unattractive, but she knew other people did; it had been a running joke since they were little. Skylar didn't know if she could be seen with him for the rest of her life. She wanted to tell herself she deserved better but knew she didn't. Skylar confessed that if she could combine Derek's looks with Emmett's personality, she'd have the perfect man.

He told her to wish in one hand and shit in the other.

Trent slid into the booth next to Jackson. He knew his friend wasn't a homophobe, but Trent still liked to fuck with him from time to time. "This seat taken?" he asked, putting his hand on Jackson's inner thigh.

Jackson jumped at the invasion of his space. "Jesus, Trent." He pushed Trent's hand away. "Keep your hands to yourself."

Emmett and Skylar sat in their side of the booth, laughing as Jackson turned red.

"Oh, you stop. You know you like it, big boy," Trent said, blowing a kiss to his friend. "Shit, I'd make your toes curl so hard they'd break."

Someone cleared their throat loudly next to the table. "Menus," the waitress said.

She looked to be pushing sixty, with a gray ponytail hanging over one shoulder. An embossed nametag hung from her stained apron. The name *'Barb'* was in white against a field of green.

"Sorry about that," Jackson said, growing even redder if that was possible. He took the offered stack of menus and passed them out.

Barb walked away, heading toward the bar. She stepped around the back and started talking to the drunk assholes.

Trent noticed a few sets of eyes head back their way. He thought the bullshit was over, but he'd seen those looks before.

"Damn, they have just about everything here," Emmett said as he flipped through the greasy, laminated pages. "Oysters? Who the fuck would get oysters out here?"

"Yeah, I'd avoid any seafood if I were you. We have a long drive ahead of us, and the last thing I want is to deal with you puking in the backseat," Skylar said without looking up from the menu.

Trenton looked over the menu but heard the sound of boots walking their way. He kept his head down, doing his best to ignore the bunch.

"You all in that little Jap shit box outside?"

They looked up at the group of men in front of their table. The one who spoke stood out from the bunch. He was young, but older than them, probably pushing thirty, if not a day or so over. His trucker hat was faded, but enough of the emblem was left to be made out.

Trent thought it was a set of tits, but it could've been headlights. Looking at the guy before him, he had every reason to believe the former.

The guy's chest was broad, and his flannel shirt was tight on his biceps. A slight gut made his shirt taut around his midsection, but he was far from fat. It was a classic beer belly, and if he didn't get a hold of his drinking soon, it would look like he swallowed a beach ball. Sandy hair poked out from under the faded cap, and a light dusting of facial hair of the same color decorated his face.

"The Toyota?" Jackson asked. "Yeah, that's my car. Why?"

Leaning on the table, the man looked each of them in the face. "You need to learn how to drive. You all almost caused an accident earlier. I don't know who the fuck taught you to drive, but stopping in the road during a snowstorm is a sure way to get killed."

Big truck, small dick, Trent thought. This asshole was the driver of the truck that almost lost control in the snow when they spoke to the cop earlier in the day. A flare of anger grew in his belly. It was warm and painful. Trenton didn't have much of a temper, but he could feel it growing by the second with this jerk blaming them for his reckless driving.

"Oh, ah, we were lost. Just getting directions is all." Jackson looked away from the bully and began looking over the menu again. He ran his finger down the selections as if trying to choose what he'd eat.

"Can we help you with anything else?" Trenton said with more than a little sass in his voice. He fluttered his eyelashes at the man.

The man's face scrunched up. "What are you, some kind of fucking faggot?" He stood straight and looked at the rest of them. "God damn, you are, aren't you?"

"Guilty, but I don't fuck peckerheads, so take your ass out of here and leave us alone."

Almost every patron in the bar gasped.

"Trent, Jesus Christ," Skylar said, looking at him.

He could see the fear in her eyes. Being gay came with its problems, but he couldn't, nor would, compare it to the sexual aggression faced by women.

"I should beat your queer ass out of here, you fucking faggot!" Spittle flew from the man's mouth, landing on the table.

"Hunter, don't waste your time with this fudge packer," another man said. He put a hand on Hunter's thick arm, trying to pull him away. "You know what your father said."

Hunter turned back to look at his friend. He sniffed and shrugged the hand off his arm. He looked at the four college students at the table, lingering on Skylar. A faux grin split his face as his eyes undressed the girl. "Nah, I'm just messing about. These folks are our guests. Right, fellas?"

A smattering of approval echoed from one man to the other.

"I would never think of starting trouble, especially with such a fine piece of ass sitting here." Hunter swung into the booth next to Skylar. He pushed her with his body, pressing her against Emmett. "Say, what's your name, darling?" Hunter threw an arm around her shoulders.

"Get your fucking hands off me!" she yelled and pushed him out of the booth onto the floor.

A few laughs rose from the drunks in the bar, but they all died instantly when the group of men glared at them.

"You fucking bitch!" Hunter stood and raised his hand.

"Do it, and I'll fucking kill you," Emmett said. He was kneeling on the seat in the booth, leaning over Skylar.

Hunter stopped as if not used to being challenged. He had the look of a spoiled kid who was finally punched in the teeth by one of his victims.

"W-what the fuck did you say to me? Huh, you ugly little shit."

Trenton slid out of the booth, allowing Jackson to exit behind him.

"Just fucking leave us alone," Jackson said.

"Or else what? Is your boyfriend gonna give us AIDS?"

"No, I'm going to put this knife in your fat neck." Trent grabbed a butter knife from the table.

"Hey!" someone yelled.

Barb walked over with an empty tray under her arm. "Cut the shit or get out." She looked at all of them, including Hunter.

"Who do you think you're talking to?" Hunter asked. "I own this fucking place."

Barb laughed. "Listen, your daddy owns this, not you. Do you want me to call him at the hotel and tell him you're harassing customers again? Huh? How will that work out?"

Biting his lower lip, Hunter stepped up to Trenton. "I'll see ya soon, fag."

Trenton's fist tightened around the butter knife. He didn't think it would do much damage to the bull of a man, but he didn't want to find out. He wasn't a killer, at least, he didn't think so. Maybe if his life was truly in danger, then maybe.

"And as for you," he leaned in close to Skylar.

She backed away, but he grabbed the back of her head, making her shriek.

The other boys tensed, but Barb raised a hand, stopping them. She shook her head just a little.

"I'm getting that pussy before you leave Braxton. One way or another." He sniffed her hair and let her go.

The group of men walked away, heading back to the bar. Even though they were gone, their eyes were still locked on the four of them.

Trent and Jackson sat back down, but Trent could see the tears welling up in Skylar's eyes.

Barb looked at the frazzled kids. "I'll give y'all a few more minutes." She walked away, heading toward Hunter and his group of friends.

"What the fuck are we going to do?" Emmett asked. "You heard what she said. That asshole's father owns the place where we're staying."

"I'm not surprised. Assholes breed assholes," Trent said. The knife was back on the table but close to his hand.

"I don't like this at all," Jackson said. He reached out and touched his sister's hand. "These guys are assholes, but what options do we have? It's a blizzard out there. I don't know when it's supposed to let up, and as good as the Toyota is, I don't know if it will make it through this much snow."

Skylar shook her head and wiped her eyes with the heels of her hands. "We have to get out of here. *Now*. I know you might think I'm being overdramatic, but none of you have to go through what a woman does. That creep is a fucking predator, and he's set his sights on me. And this small-town bullshit will protect him, especially if his daddy has money. How many campus rapes were swept under the rug for a donor's son? More than you know."

"You don't know that, Sky," Jackson said.

Rage washed over her face. "Yes, I fucking do. You're not a girl. You don't hear the crying coming from a bathroom stall at night. You've never had to watch a girl almost kill herself after an abortion, thanks to an asshole forcing himself on her. You don't have to feel the shame of getting drunk and passed around like a fucking sex doll." She looked at each of them with tears in her eyes. "I'm fucking leaving with or without you." Skylar stood up.

"Fuck," Jackson said as Trenton stood.

The four of them put their coats on and bundled up against the snow, which blew hard against the windows.

"Hey, where ya going?" Hunter yelled. His speech was slurred and his eyes were glassy, but there was malice in his voice. "You and I have a date later, sweet tits." He winked at her. "Don't you forget it. And don't worry, Pop will give me a key to your room, so don't wait up."

The men around him laughed and slapped him on the back. Some of them even made lewd oral sex gestures at her.

Together, the friends fled the restaurant and

jumped into the car. Jackson started it up, using the wipers to clear the windshield. He turned the heat on high, but none of them could seem to get warm.

CHAPTER 14

Human meat roasted over the open flames of the fireplace. The smell was intoxicating, and the Runts couldn't wait to eat. It had been years since they had human flesh; not since Pickles died and they risked eating him.

Rocky walked up close to Hammer, getting near the fire. "Can't wait to have a bite of that."

Hammer looked down on her.

The patches of brown scales on her face reflected the firelight.

"And where the fuck were you during the hunt? Even Bags and Bull helped, and he can't even see. What were you doing, playing nurse to the fucking baby?"

Rocky backed away from the massive mutant. She heard what he'd done out there, how he fucked the dead woman, splitting her damn near in half.

It was hard to ignore when they brought the desecrated corpse back. The gaping hole where her pussy and asshole used to reside was a mess of ripped flesh and every fluid imaginable.

Rocky knew she had to do something to win over Hammer or she might go hungry. He'd already blown a load, so he wasn't thinking with his cock, at least, not at that moment. She put her arm around his massive waist. "No, baby, I was cutting up the remains of the deer." It was a lie, but she had to think of something. The Runts had picked the animal almost clean, and she knew it.

"Must've been a quick job considering that thing was pretty much bones when we were done."

The fire hissed and popped as fat dripped onto the flames.

"Ah, that should be cooked enough." He pulled the chunk of meat from the fireplace with metal tongs and put it directly on the wooden table and cut a piece from it with his knife.

The human meat still dripped gore, but he didn't care. Hammer shoved the wet chunk into his mouth. His crooked teeth mashed the meat to a pulp before he swallowed it.

Bags was on the ground with a hacksaw and cleaver. She crudely butchered both of the corpses, stripping what meat she could from them.

The rest of the Runts, who lived in the outbuildings around the main house, piled in. They drooled and moaned, limping around to get a cut of fresh meat. It was something rare for them, and their malnourished bodies showcased that fact.

As much as Hammer wanted to tell them to fuck off, he knew he couldn't. They were family. He just wished Grammy would stop taking in more mouths to feed.

The baby was young and had to live off milk, but

soon, she'd be old enough to eat their food. Good food was already scarce.

He might have to have one of his siblings fall victim to an 'accident' sooner or later. That would eliminate an extra stomach to fill and give them more to eat. While he liked tit fucking Bags, if he could somehow take her and Bull out, they'd be in meat for a while.

Hammer pushed the uneaten portion of meat to the side, letting Rocky have it. "Here."

She shrieked and began ripping at the chunk of flesh.

He watched them all eat, growing full on the fresh food, but it wouldn't last. Soon, they'd be starving again, scrounging roots and small game. They needed more. They needed to hunt, and hunt often, even if it meant occasionally grabbing one or two of the townsfolk.

"God damn, Hammer, this pussy meat tastes great," Froggy said. "We had to rinse it pretty good and trim the hair from it, but what was left is damn tasty." He put a shredded piece of vagina skin in his mouth and ate. His face was swollen, but the joy he showed eating the dead woman made up for the injuries.

Hammer nodded, and Froggy walked back into the fray of the other Runts. "Where's Grammy?" he asked Rocky, who was licking juices from her brown fingers.

"She's in the back room with the baby. She said she didn't want to be disturbed, so you'll have to wait."

Hammer huffed. And just like that, he felt as if he were replaced, pushed by the wayside by a toothless freak. A freak that couldn't even contribute to their family, at least, by helping. She *could* make a meal, albeit a small one. He wanted to talk to the matriarch of the family to get her permission to hunt again, but Hammer was over that notion. No person, no matter who they were, should be able to tell someone else how to survive. He walked through the crowd finding the biggest and smartest of the Runts. He gathered them all up, making sure Rocky couldn't slip away.

"What's going on?" Glump asked. His face was streaked with blood and rendered fat.

Hammer looked down at all of them. His mutated face threw off his vision when he looked down too long. "We're going hunting again. Kill whoever we find, regardless of whether they're townsfolk or not. Grammy can live on pine needle tea and root stew. We're young and hungry. We need meat if we're gonna survive the winter."

A sea of monstrous faces looked back at him. Cleft palates looked alien as they broke into crude smiles. Rheumy eyes wept milky fluid, and deformed hands clenched into fists.

"I'm going back out and need you all to come with me."

They all nodded and grabbed whatever weapons they could find.

Together, as a freakish family, they set back out into the storm.

CHAPTER 15

Jackson did everything he could to keep the compact car on the snowy road. He could hardly see through the rapidly falling snow.

The Toyota struggled through deep drifts, which were higher than the bumper.

Using a low gear, Jackson kept the engine RPMs high as he did his best to keep the car moving forward.

The GPS was little help. They had a route out of the area, but the time to their destination increased with every passing second. Multiple road closures, some reported, others not, caused them to detour numerous times.

"This was a bad fucking idea," Jackson said. His brow was damp, and his crotch and armpits were wet with fear sweat.

The car slid again, and he hoped it would stay on the road. Faster and faster, the wipers moved, clearing the windshield. He'd rather do 90 MPH on the highway than 20 MPH in the snow.

"Staying at that place wasn't an option anymore.

We had to leave, even if it means pulling over and camping for the night in the car. At least we're away from them," Skylar said. Her eyes were red, but she'd stopped crying long ago.

"Agreed, hun," Trent said. He clutched his seatbelt tight as if that would help him in any way. "Those guys were not worth the trouble. A bunch of fucking assholes. I'd much rather make this drive than deal with them."

Jackson checked his mirrors out of habit.

They hadn't seen many vehicles since leaving Braxton. A few plows were on the road, but they were fighting an uphill battle with the steady snowfall. Jackson would give his left nut for a plow to be ahead of them clearing a path, but there was none—just them and his little car.

It felt like they'd been driving for hours, but it hadn't even been one. The detours and turnarounds had them backtracking and confused, and they weren't the only ones messed up by the closures. The GPS was having difficulty keeping up with the ever-changing traffic pattern.

Taking another reflexive check in his rearview, Jackson did a double take. In the darkness of the night, two headlights cut through the gloom. "Fuck, we have company."

The other three passengers turned and looked as the vehicle sped up, closing the distance.

"Fuck, is it them?" Emmett asked. He tried to make out the vehicle, but only seeing the lights did little to help him.

The lights grew closer. It was a bigger vehicle, either an SUV or truck based on the height.

"No, it can't be," Skylar said. "They were happy

and drunk back at the bar. Why the hell would they drive out here? We're no one." A look of fear came over her face.

Jackson knew Hunter had said something crude to his sister when he walked away. He couldn't tell what it was but knew it was terrible. Even when they got going, she refused to tell them.

The big vehicle moved closer.

"Oh shit, it's them," Emmett said. "Fuck. What are we going to do?"

They looked back at the truck nearing their bumper.

"We just keep driving and hope they turn around. I'm sure they're just out here to give us a scare." Jackson didn't even believe his voice.

"Fucking leave us alone," Trenton said, even though the occupants of the truck clearly couldn't hear him.

They all screamed as the truck's bumper made contact with the Toyota's.

"Oh shit!" Jackson yelled as he lost control of the car.

It spun and spun, heading toward the trees.

***

"I told that little slut her pussy would be mine," Hunter said from behind the wheel of the truck. "And that fucking bitch, Barb, thinking she can threaten me? Let's see if that skank still has a job in the morning. My father isn't gonna stand for some fucking waitress threatening a Shield."

The Toyota came to a stop when it struck a tree. Plastic cracked and metal bent on impact. Smoke rose from underneath the car's hood.

Hunter saw movement inside. His big truck crawled to a halt, lighting up the car's interior with its headlights. He took the bottle of Evan Williams from the center console and gulped, then wiped his mouth with his sleeve and handed the bottle to Garrett, who sat shotgun.

Garrett took the bottle and drank.

Both men were already fucked up from drinking earlier, but it didn't feel right to take that drive without a fresh bottle to keep them company.

After the teens left, Hunter told everyone he was calling it a night.

Some people believed him, but others didn't, and almost no one cared except Garrett. He had his eyes on the girl from the moment she walked in. From the shadows of the bar, he drank with a few buddies, but his attention was no longer on them. His eyes were glued to her, and for good reason. She looked just like the first girl he raped after working at Romano's carnival.

He'd just dropped out of high school the summer before, and the traveling show allowed him to get out of Braxton. It wasn't world travel, or even national travel, but it got him out of his mother's shitty trailer.

Dealing with her was a nightmare, but his stepfather was the devil. Always drunk and pissed, he was either fighting or fucking, and sometimes both if his mother was unlucky. She'd never leave him, though. Garrett knew, one day, she'd turn up dead at his stepfather's hands.

The carnival was great—easy work, tons of free food, and lots of pussy walking around. When he saw her, he thought she was the best-looking girl he'd ever laid eyes on.

Garrett did his best to strike up a conversation with her while she waited in line for his ride, but after she called him trailer trash and laughed in his face, he knew his chances were over. Well, his chances at a legit fuck, anyway.

He found her wandering the grassy parking lot, which was in disarray thanks to the teens they had parking the cars. After donning a mask and preemptively putting a condom on, Garrett struck. He kept the knife to her throat to keep her from screaming. The only thing he heard was the raucous sound of the carnival and his rough breath through the rubber clown mask.

That was over ten years ago, but like with anything, you never forget your first.

"You're gonna let me break a piece of that ass off, right?" Garrett asked. He took a pack of smokes from his vest pocket and lit one without asking.

Hunter looked over at him, ready to bitch about the smoking, but there was something in the way Garrett stared at him; something that chilled even Hunter. Right then, he realized bringing the man was a mistake. "Yeah, but you get sloppy seconds."

Garrett didn't speak, but slightly nodded. "What about the others? Them boys are probably pussies, but it's three on two. And the one is pretty big and young."

"Well, one of them is a faggot, so unless he scratches our eyes out, we should be fine. The other two won't be a problem. Not if they want to walk away from this."

"Oh, how so?" Garrett asked with his cigarette dangling from his lip.

Hunter smiled and reached behind his seat. His

hands came out holding a sawed-off pump shotgun. He racked it, chambering a shell. "This is how I know."

Garrett smiled and opened the door. "Shall we?"

CHAPTER 16

Grammy did her best to keep the baby quiet; she'd been fed and changed, but still, the little one fussed. "Shh," Grammy cooed, rocking the newborn in her thin arms.

The baby wriggled but didn't cry. Her misshapen mouth twitched and curled into a yawn.

A loud yell came from the other room and the Runts cheered.

The baby's mouth went from a yawn to a scream.

"Fuck," Grammy muttered. She rocked the screaming baby in her arms, hoping the damn Runts would quiet down soon. As tempting as it was to go out there and tell them to knock it off, she knew they needed the bonding time. She assumed the hunt had gone well, which was the reason for the celebration.

There was still some of the venison Hammer brought her, and she'd make it last. Growing up piss poor, Grammy had eaten her fair share of disgusting foods, but human flesh wasn't something she could stomach.

When Pickles died, she knew his meat would get

them by. That was years ago when their numbers were slightly lower and they had younger mouths to feed. Now, most of her Runts were adults or teenagers with even bigger appetites.

Another yell sounded out followed by more whooping.

Grammy heard a sound like a stampede, and the front door slammed shut.

The baby screamed again, but something didn't feel right.

There was just something not sitting well with Grammy. She'd lived in that house for her entire life, and with the rejected youth of a polluted town for the last twenty-plus years. Each Runt was special to her, and she knew them intimately.

She put the screaming infant down on a pile of blankets on her thin mattress, ensuring there was enough to keep the child from moving too much.

"What's all the yelling about?" she asked, walking into the room.

Two human corpses sat on the table, the flesh almost picked clean from them. The smell of cooked meat hung in the air.

She looked around, taking a quick headcount of those remaining.

Some of the Runts lived in the outbuildings on the property, but many lived with her. With the blowing snow and darkness, Grammy didn't think many of them would be outside. She was confident they would all be turning in for the night, especially after eating such a large meal.

"Where's Hammer?" she asked no one in particular. "And Froggy, Glump, and Rocky are missing too. Where are they?"

The remaining Runts looked anywhere but at her.

She scanned the room, looking for any others who may have gone on the hunt from earlier. By the fire, she saw Bull and Bags warming themselves.

Bags tended to the fire underneath a battered pot.

Bull's stomach would sometimes get upset if he overate, so his sister would brew him tea. The big, bald mutant sat eyeless by the fire. The lack of other senses enhanced his sense of touch.

Bags turned her gaze as Grammy's eyes met hers.

Something was wrong.

"Bags, where the hell is Hammer and the others?" She put her hands on her hips and looked down at the legless, three-fingered girl. "And don't you lie to me. I'll know it if you do."

Bags delayed using a metal hook to pull the pot from the hanger above the fire. She poured some water into a tin cup and the spicy aroma of pine needle tea wafted up with the steam. "Want some?" she asked.

"No, but put it back on the fire. I'll need hot water for the baby's milk in a little while. Now, tell me where they went."

Bags sighed and looked toward the front door.

Grammy snapped her head and moved to the front window.

Black shapes, big and small, ran through the snow toward the road. They were going on another hunt!

She couldn't allow it. It was already bad enough she let them take the two people on the table. She prayed they weren't locals, just travelers who got lost in the snow.

Grammy pulled the door open and was met with a gust of snowy wind. "Hammer! Get back here."

The wind pulled the words from her lips and blew

them away. But then, she saw the big, misshapen form of her oldest child slow, but he didn't turn. "Hammer!" she yelled again. Grammy knew he heard her but didn't turn back.

A loud bang echoed through the night.

A car accident.

The Runts in the yard yelled and shouted, picking up their pace as they pushed through the snow toward the sound of another meal.

CHAPTER 17

The roar of the shotgun was loud, sounding out of place in the snowstorm. The short barrel spat fire and buckshot into the air.

Hunter's ears were ringing, but he wanted the kids to know he wasn't fucking around. They could do as he said, or he'd leave them for dead. It was that simple.

"We just want the girl. That's it. Let us have some quick fun with her and we'll be out of your hair. Hell, we'll even give you a ride back into town. That little tin can of a car ain't going anywhere now. Do what we say and you'll make it out alive. If not, well, I don't think I have to explain myself any further."

There was movement in the car, but no one exited the vehicle.

"It's fucking cold out here, kiddies," Garrett said. "The longer you make us wait, the worse it's gonna be."

He started walking toward the car in the trees and shined a flashlight through the foggy glass. He felt like he was in the butcher shop picking out a favorite steak, but he already knew what he was craving. His eyes were locked on the girl in the backseat. He never noticed the mutated shapes moving through the woods.

***

"Is everyone okay?" Jackson asked.

The car was totaled, but somehow the airbags didn't deploy.

He felt a burn on his neck from the seatbelt, but other than that, he was fine. At least physically.

"I-I fucked my knee up," Emmett said. Even in the dark, the swelling on his leg was evident. "I don't think it's broken, but if I have to run, that's gonna be a problem."

"What the fuck are we going to do?" Trenton asked. He had a few bumps, but nothing as pressing as the two psychos armed with a gun.

"I don't know! I don't know!" Skylar shrieked. She couldn't take her eyes off the men. Even through the glass, she could hear their demands. Being defiled by them was a nightmare. She'd rather them put that gun in her mouth and blow her head off. That might still happen, but not before they had their way with her.

"They want Skylar," Emmett said, gripping his swollen leg. "Look, they're going to take her anyway."

The others looked at him like he had three heads.

"What the fuck does that mean?" Jackson snapped. "We're not giving my sister to those fucks. I'd rather die than let that happen."

"I know, I know. I'm not saying that, but…"

"But what? What are you saying?" Trenton asked.

Emmett looked at Skylar who had a fresh batch of tears in her eyes and a hurt look on her face.

A flashlight illuminated the interior of the car.

Emmett could feel the hatred of his three friends, one of whom he wanted to share a life with. He regretted what he said the instant it came out of his mouth, but it was the truth. Their only chance at survival was Skylar. Even if the men left them alone, they'd surely freeze to death without the car's heat. It was their only option if they wanted to live.

Skylar followed the beam of light as it approached the car. She could see the man's face and realized she didn't recognize him. It wasn't Hunter, which meant he was the one with the gun.

The man looked at her like she was food—prey—and he was the predator.

Skylar wouldn't scream no matter what they did to her. She wouldn't allow it.

Something moved in the dark behind the man, but his attention was solely on her. He didn't hear the monster emerging from the woods.

In the moonlight, Skylar saw the axe flash.

In seconds, she broke the promise she'd made to herself.

She screamed.

CHAPTER 18

Hammer swung the axe in a downward arc like he was splitting firewood. But instead of wood, the blade split a human skull.

The steel cleaved through the man's head with a wet thud. The wide base of the axe opened his cranium with brutal efficiency, exposing the brain matter to the snow.

Snowflakes fell, as did a steady drip of gore. Only the man's jawbone stopped the axe from continuing south.

Twisting the handle, Hammer cracked the tiny fragments of the ruined skull as he tried to dislodge the axe. His victim's left eye popped free and dangled on his cheek when Hammer yanked on the stuck weapon.

A blast like thunder sounded to his left.

Something stung his flank, and the back window of the car shattered in a flurry of broken glass.

With a grunt and final tug, Hammer pulled the axe free and turned to look at the man holding the shotgun.

The armed man was no traveler, but a local for

sure. There was something familiar about him.

The boy in the truck! He was the one I beat up all those years ago. And still, he doesn't fight fair. Hammer's mind flashed back to when the boy and his friends destroyed one of their fields.

The man racked the shotgun, expelling the smoking shell into the deep snow.

Hammer had no fear of death. It was something not in his mind. Every day could be his last.

None of them knew the lifespan of the Runts. For all they knew, their mutations were ticking bombs just waiting to go off.

The man leveled the shotgun at Hammer's chest. A black maw stared at him, and he didn't even flinch, knowing what would happen.

Something moved past Hammer, rushing toward the man with the gun.

Glump!

The crazy fuck charged at the man with something in his hand. It was a pile of his mushy shit.

When they were moving through the woods, Glump disappeared for a moment. Hammer now knew why.

The gunman turned his aim away from Hammer, pointing the shotgun at the charging mutant.

Glump threw the wad of shit at the man as the gun fired. His throw was low, hitting his victim in the chest.

This time, the shotgun blast was on target, catching the mutant full on in the belly. Some of the pellets missed Glump, but more than enough hit him, turning his torso into a red slurry.

The errant shots flew past Hammer like angry bees. He knew he had to act fast before the man reloaded the big gun.

Without pause, the man racked the gun, feeding a fresh shell into the chamber. Then, he aimed again; this time, Hammer was closer as he charged in.

Roaring, holding the axe high, Hammer was ready to kill or be killed.

Another scream burst through the night air: the scream of the gunman.

Glump's shit ate through the man's heavy coat, burning away the skin of his chest. He swatted at the acidic mess, only doing more damage as his fingers bubbled and burned.

The shotgun was all but forgotten as the man fell onto the snow, trying his best to quell the chemical burns.

Hammer rushed and raised the axe.

The man put up his hand in his last moments to try and stop the blow, but Hammer changed the angle of his attack, swinging the axe in a low arc. The blade took the man in the armpit, biting deep into the flesh.

Blood sprayed as an artery was severed. Snow turned red with the ruined arm flapping freely.

This time, the axe didn't get stuck in the victim. Hammer ripped it back, throwing a fan of blood in its wake.

The man didn't have time to beg as the weapon began its arc again. Heavy steel bit through the soft muscle and blood vessels of his neck. More gore rushed out, melting the snow around him. His eyes stayed open as Hammer pulled the axe free.

The remaining Runts swarmed the car, the meat inside screaming into the night.

Smiling, Hammer joined his siblings.

***

"What the fuck!" Jackson screamed at seeing the mutated girl with skin that looked like stone.

She broke his window with a rock, sending glass into his face.

"Ah!" Jackson screamed as glass blinded him. He kicked the door open, striking the girl. His vision was nearly gone, but he could see enough to throw a punch. He swung with every bit of force he could muster, striking the mutant in the face. Her rough skin cut his knuckles, but he felt the rewarding crunch of a bone breaking. He didn't know if it was her nose or cheek, but he hurt the bitch.

"Run! Everyone fucking run!" Jackson screamed.

Something struck him in the belly, knocking the wind out of him. The fist pulled back and hit him again and again.

Through his injured eyes, Jackson realized he wasn't getting punched; he was being stabbed.

The freak's nose was bent sideways from his punch. Blood ran down her face, turning her stone flesh into a disturbing mask of gore. She smiled as she thrust the short knife into his gut again.

Jackson could smell his perforated intestines. Warm blood ran down his stomach, wetting his crotch. He stumbled forward, pushing her, hoping to keep his feet under him. Within two steps, Jackson stumbled and landed in the snow.

The freak jumped on his back, and the last thing he felt was the cold bite of the blade as it was pulled across his throat.

***

Back in their travels, Trenton didn't know if he could kill another human being, but that notion went by the wayside as he watched the freakish girl slit Jackson's throat. He rounded the car, knowing there was a gun somewhere.

When he was younger, his father took him shooting to try and 'get the gay out of his son.' It didn't work, but Trenton was fascinated with the firearms. Since then, he'd been shooting a few times but wasn't as good as he could be. Still, he knew his way around a shotgun.

A squat-looking freak with bulging eyes swung a crude club at his face.

Trent ducked, feeling the turbulence of the weapon miss him by a mere inch. He punched the freak in the gut and heard the gasp of wind knocked from his lungs. Scrambling in the snow on his hands and knees, he regained his footing.

The big freak who killed Hunter and his passenger was moving toward the driver's side of the vehicle. He looked into the car with his deformed face.

Emmett and Skylar were still in there, facing down the axe-wielding monster.

Trenton needed to get to the gun. It was the only chance any of them had at survival.

A chorus of screams came from the back of the car as the monster shattered the back window.

With the rear windshield demolished, it was easy for Trenton to watch the scene unfold.

Steam rose from the spilled blood around Hunter's corpse. But next to his mangled body lay salvation: the shotgun.

Picking up the heavy weapon, Trenton relished in the warmth radiating from the freshly fired barrel. He did his best to aim the sawed-off gun at the behemoth attacking his friends, but he was too scared of hitting one of them in the process.

The freak with the bulging eyes charged at him, holding his cudgel above his head. He screamed angrily, making his eyes wider than anything Trenton had ever seen.

Trent's eyes flashed back and forth to the big freak still by the car and the smaller one rushing him. He knew he should use his shot to kill the bigger one, but there was still no clear target. The smaller freak was closing in, nearly within arm's reach. Without a moment to spare, Trent pointed the gun and fired.

The mutant was too close for him to miss. All the pellets from the buckshot caught the wide-eyed freak in the face, blowing his head apart. A pink mist hung in the air as the monster's forward momentum carried him. He fell dead in the snow at Trent's feet, landing next to Hunter.

Trent cycled the action of the gun, praying for one more shot—one more chance to take down the giant. He opened the action, sending the spent casing spinning into the snow. His heart sank when he saw the weapon was empty.

Something hummed through the air, and he looked up just in time to see the axe flying end-over-end toward him. He tried to use the gun to block it, but missed. The head of the blade caught him in the chest, knocking him to his ass.

It felt like he had a truck on his ribcage, crushing all the breath from him. Blood oozed up from his throat. He belched a crimson bubble, popping all over his face.

The massive mutant rushed him, looking down at

the one Trenton killed with his final shotgun shell. He reached down and grabbed the axe's handle, stepping on Trent's crotch, using the leverage to pull the weapon free.

Looking up at the night sky, Trenton did his best not to make eye contact with the horrors above him. Snow fell on him in a silent cascade of white. He was cold. More of his warm blood spurted from his mouth as he stared at the white glow of the moon hidden behind thick clouds.

The last thing he saw was the axe blade as it descended toward his face.

***

Emmett was going to die; this was the end for him. He needed to get the fuck out of the car and away from the carnage.

The mutant that was trying to pull him from the car took off when the blast of the gun ripped through the night air.

It was his only chance for escape, but he didn't know what to do about Skylar. He didn't want to leave her alone, but if they both stayed, they were as good as dead.

He kicked open his door, doing his best to ignore Jackson's ruined body near his feet.

"Go, go, go," Skylar yelled. She had her door open with the same idea as him. The only difference was she was facing the patch of woods where the freaks came from. If she doubled back and around the car, she'd alert them.

The big one was preoccupied with mutilating the body of Trenton, who was being hacked to a pulp.

Emmett found strength in his wounded leg, relying on pure adrenaline to fuel him. He limped out in the direction of the freakish woman with stone-like skin. She was the one who killed Jackson, and she still held the blade wet with his blood in her hand.

Emmett wasn't much of a fighter, but he was bigger than the freak.

She swiped at his face with the knife, flaying open his cheek.

The cut didn't hurt at first, but the coolness of the night air hit his back molars as the flap of his face fell open. He didn't have time to be in shock. This was do or die.

She wound up again, thrusting toward his gut like she'd done to Jackson.

Emmett stepped to the side and grabbed her scaly wrist. Her skin was hard and textured, like rough asphalt. He yanked her forward and headbutted her in her already broken nose. His head rang from the strike, but he knew the damage he'd inflicted was much worse.

Her hand went slack, and the knife fell.

Reaching down, Emmett grabbed it by the blade, slicing his palm, but at least he was armed. He let the dazed mutant go and switched the grip on the knife, holding it by the handle. Without a second thought, he plunged it into the freak's chest. Before releasing the grip, he felt the tip of the blade flutter as it pierced her heart.

The girl collapsed, reaching for the blade that ended her life.

A roar sounded behind him. He invoked the rage of the massive beast.

Emmett ran with everything he had, hobbling into

the woods. A *whoosh* sounded next to him as the axe sailed past his head and into a tree. The handle quivered and vibrated but failed to hit its mark.

It didn't matter; Emmett couldn't outrun the mutant. He tripped over a downed log, landing in the snow. His sliced palm burned and stung, but he pushed that away with his adrenaline. Risking a glance behind him, he knew the giant would pursue him to finish the job.

A scream echoed, and he turned just in time to see the freak, and a few others, grab Skylar. They wrapped a thick cord of rope around her wrists as she fought.

The giant punched her in the face with a crack, knocking her out, then threw her over his shoulder like she was nothing more than a toddler. The monster looked into the dark trees where Emmett hid like a coward and smiled.

Other freaks emerged from the trees and gathered the corpses of his friends and the two men who attacked them.

As if they'd never been there, the freaks melted into the darkness with Skylar as their hostage, dragging the dead behind them like a macabre parade.

CHAPTER 19

Hammer burst into the cabin with the girl over his shoulder. During his trek back to the house, she'd come to.

She began biting and kicking as soon as she regained consciousness, doing her best to get free.

He was tempted to kill her then and there, but restrained himself. He wanted to do it his way. This time, he'd split a living pussy with his cock, watching as he fucked her life away. He didn't know when he'd get another chance, and he already squandered one that night. He couldn't do it again.

The Runts in the cabin jumped up as the hunting party stormed in. They whooped and cheered seeing the four adult corpses they dragged along behind them. With the freezing weather, they could preserve the meat for the rest of winter, possibly saving their lives.

Hammer threw the girl on the blood-stained table and used more rope to tie her down. He took his knife and cut her clothes away, leaving her cold and naked.

"This one has a bald pussy," he said, admiring her

pink slit. "She sure as hell isn't a kid, that's for sure." He put his mushed nose against her vagina and sniffed. "Mmm, smells scared and stinky." His grotesque tongue uncurled from his mouth and ran the length of her, starting with her puckered anus and ending with a slurp on her hooded clitoris. "Tastes as good as it looks."

"Hey, Hammer, can I get a taste?" Shroom asked. He was short and lumpy, covered in mushroom-like growths. They covered most of his body, including his face. He wandered closer to the girl, licking the growths on his lips.

Hammer swung at him but missed. "Stay the fuck back. My dick is already fucked up enough. I don't need any of your growths on it."

"Awe, come on, Hammer. You know that shit ain't catching. Just a lick. Or if not, maybe a sniff?"

Other Runts stood around Shroom with looks of hope on their deformed faces. The only pussy they'd ever had or seen had belonged to their fellow mutants. It was the first time many of them had seen a clean, healthy woman.

"Fine, you can smell her, but if your tongue comes out, I swear on everything I'll cut it off."

Shroom nodded and dove into the girl's crotch. His nose got as close as possible without making contact with her moist slit.

One after another, the Runts took turns smelling the girl.

When Hammer's back was turned, Crow slid his tongue into her asshole.

The others yelled jealously, but when Hammer looked, they all played dumb. At least one of them tasted the girl before Hammer had his way with her.

"You, you, you, and you," Hammer pointed to four Runts. "Go back to the road and collect our dead. We lost three out there, but their meat is still good. Can't let nothing go to waste."

Each assigned Runts grabbed whatever outerwear they could find and bundled up. They grabbed the rope to make the drag easier.

Crow, whose face was covered in black hair that looked like fine feathers, didn't want to leave the house. He kept sniffing his hairy upper lip, savoring the smell of the girl's cunt. But he knew disobeying Hammer wasn't wise, and it was better to get the meat as he'd get a prime cut when the time came.

"Let's get out there and back before Hammer starts the show." Crow opened the door and stopped.

A wet crack echoed in the room.

He fell back, dead, with an axe stuck in his face.

***

Emmett felt like a coward for not doing anything to save Skylar. After sitting in the woods for a few minutes, he knew he had to do something. He couldn't stay in the cold; that was just as much of a death sentence as going after his love.

He pulled the axe out of the tree with some exertion and luck. The head of it was tacky with the gore from Trenton, but he pushed that notion from his mind. His friends were dead, but one of them still lived—the one he loved.

The mutants were easy to follow, even in the blowing snow. Their footprints were like neon signs in the woods, not to mention the gory streaks left behind by the dragged corpses.

His journey was painful and tough, as his knee was grotesquely swollen. The adrenaline dump had worn off, leaving him tired and scared. He didn't have much of a plan, but he had to try to pick the mutants off individually, hopefully ambushing them, especially the giant. He was a mean son of a bitch, and Emmett knew he'd be hard to kill.

Slinking up to the house, he used the shadows for cover. He gasped when he saw the giant licking Skylar's vagina through the window. The revulsion on her face was palatable. Emmett cringed seeing the violation of her body.

The other freaks lined up, but the big one was arguing with them.

Emmett couldn't hear what was said, but it looked like he was turning them down for whatever they'd requested.

After a few more moments, the giant nodded, and the others took turns putting their faces between Skylar's legs. They didn't lick her; it looked like they were smelling her.

One of the freaks—this one covered in what looked like black feathers—stole a quick taste when the big one wasn't looking.

Emmett's pulse raced, and he tightened his numb grip on the axe. The cut on his hand burned, but the pain felt good. It reminded him he was still alive. His face had gone numb from the cold, but he could feel the wind on his exposed teeth. The slice on his cheek flapped when he moved.

Without warning, the big one began shouting orders, and Emmett pulled himself away from the window, pressing his back against the cabin.

A group of the freaks were throwing on jackets,

meaning they'd soon be coming back outside.

His knee throbbed in agony. There was no way he could run and hide again. Besides, he didn't know how much more of the cold he could take before his body stopped working. If he was going to make a stand, it had to be then.

Adjusting his grip on the axe, Emmett took a deep breath as the door opened.

He stepped into the light pouring from the door and swung.

CHAPTER 20

Skylar was going to die. She was cold even with the fireplace roaring not far from her. It wasn't the cold of the room, but the chill she felt in her core. She knew she was doomed, and her death wouldn't come easy. There was no hope, no prayer for a rescue. Her brother was dead, and both of her friends as well.

She thought about her family and what they'd think. Would they ever find out the grisly truth, or would they hope that their children would return one day? She even thought about Emmett and how she'd treated him. He didn't deserve what she put him through. He wasn't built like a model, like Derek, but he was a great guy. He always had been, but something about him wouldn't let her fall in love with him. Even with her death looming, she couldn't see herself living life with him by her side. Yes, he was safe, loyal, and an above-average lover, but she didn't love him, not like that, and she never could. She wished she would've told him that instead of giving him the cold shoulder all these months.

Skylar felt dirty. Not for what she did to Emmett, but physically. Her vagina was wet and cold, and it wasn't due to excitement. The disgusting saliva of the freaks coated her like slime, something repulsive, like the remnants of a drain trap. It was only a matter of time before they killed her.

A group of the freaks were getting dressed and preparing to go back out into the cold. Deep in her chest, an ember of hope burned. Maybe Emmett escaped and found help, and the mutants were going out to meet an army of cops. They'd all die in a hail of gunfire before the boys in blue broke in and rescued her.

"You know what he's going to do to you, right?"

Turning her head, Skylar saw two freaks standing next to her. The male was massive and fat, like a giant baby. He had no ears, eyes, or nose, and a mouth that didn't look like it was accustomed to speaking. A pair of floppy breasts hung over his shoulders, and her eyes followed them to their owner.

On the freak's back was a deformed girl who only had three fingers on each hand. She was mutated, but there was a sense of intelligence in her eyes, something Skylar didn't think she'd find in that hell hole.

"He's gonna fuck you to death. We call him Hammer, not for the size of his body, but for his freakish cock. He's gonna split that bald little pussy wide open. You seem like a nice girl, so I thought I'd let you know. I don't know if that's a blessing or a curse, but you should know what awaits you."

Skylar licked her lips. "Please, when they leave, untie me. I promise I won't tell a soul what happened here, honest."

The girl on the back of the freak pulled a crude set

of reins attached to the big one's mouth who lowered himself so the girl could look Skylar in the eyes.

"Ha! Imagine that. I couldn't do it if I wanted to. This is a rough time of year for us, all of us. You and your friends aren't people to us. You're food. And we need meat to make it through the winter. Yes, he's going to fuck you to death, but after that, we're gonna cut you up and freeze your flesh." She rubbed Skylar's sweaty brow with her deformed hand. "Hopefully, for your sake, you die quickly. I've seen what he can do with that thing, and it ain't pretty."

They both looked up as the door opened.

Skylar saw Emmett step into the doorway for a fraction of a second. He was bloody and cold, with his cheek hanging by a flap. But it wasn't his injuries she focused on, it was the axe he held in his hand.

In the blink of an eye, Emmett swung the axe, driving it into the skull of the hairy freak who licked her asshole.

He fell back into the cabin, dead. Blood poured from his skull as the rest of the freaks rushed out into the dark chasing Emmett.

Skylar said a little prayer for her friend, and right then and there, she vowed that if they made it out alive, she'd give him a chance—a real chance, not just a one-night stand. He came back for her. He was her only hope.

Suddenly, Skylar was alone. All the freaks fled into the night, hunting her friend who'd killed one of them. The sound of the fire was the only company she had besides the corpse with the axe in its face.

Her arms and legs burned from the coarse rope wrapped around them. But she noticed something. The bindings were a little loose.

CHAPTER 21

Hammer's emotions ran wild. The boy who so brazenly killed Crow limped in the snow, trying his best to keep watch on the swarming mutants. He hated the boy, but part of him wanted to thank him. Not only had he dwindled their numbers, meaning food would go further, but he added to their meat total.

With the deaths of the other Runts, the rest of them would have enough meat to see them through a good portion of the year. But, on the other hand, he killed his kin—men and women with whom he'd grown up, laughed with, and shared the same struggles. Hammer may have been grateful for the new source of food, but it didn't change the fact the boy had to die. And die horribly.

"Kill him!" Hammer screamed at the rest of his family.

Two of the Runts rushed the boy, seeking an easy kill and getting on the good graces of Hammer. They both froze when the boy pulled the shotgun from behind him.

"Stay back, or I'll blow your fucking heads off." He pointed the big gun at them, causing the first two to stop dead in their tracks.

They looked at each other, thinking the other should rush first and the second would catch the boy during his reload.

"Kill him!" Hammer bellowed again. "The fucking thing is empty. If it weren't, he would've used it already."

The look of realization on the boy's face was the only reassurance the two mutants needed. They rushed him.

The boy raised the shotgun as if he were going to fire, causing the charging Runts to slow. It was just enough time for him to adjust his grip on the gun, holding it by the barrel. He swung it like a club, catching one of them in the temple.

The Runt, whose head was just as deformed as Hammer's, fell in a heap. Blood ran from his fractured skull as he dropped in the deep snow.

The second Runt, Clubber, whose left hand had no fingers, charged. He screamed, showing his few remaining teeth.

The boy didn't have enough time to wind up for another blow. He dropped the gun in the snow and pulled a knife from his belt.

Hammer recognized the blade. It belonged to Rocky, and he'd last seen it stuck in her chest.

The boy ducked as Clubber swung his meaty fist and struck, thrusting the short blade into the mutant's gut.

Clubber shrieked as the boy slid the blade up his stomach, spilling his guts. Thick ropes of intestines and putrid stomach matter fell, steaming into the snow. The mortally wounded Runt collapsed, doing his best to hold in his ruined innards.

Tang, a squat Runt with arms that hung to the ground, stepped up next to Hammer and cocked his long arm back. He held a crude spear made of a branch with a blade formed from an old shovel head.

The weapon flew through the air, nearly invisible in the dark.

With a gasp and scream, the boy shouted as the spear burrowed into his upper thigh. "Fuck!" Blood seeped from around the blade. The boy put both hands on the shaft, trying to free it. He fell into the snow as the rest of the Runts, sensing the kill, charged.

A handful of mutated faces, too short or too long limbs, oozing sores, and freakish cries rushed in.

The boy tried to stand and run, but the fight was out of him. He pulled the spear from his leg, unleashing even more blood from the wound.

Holding the weapon before him, the boy prepared his last stand.

Hammer was impressed. Not too impressed, the kid still had to die, but enough to admire the defeated foe.

***

Emmett immediately regretted not stealing Hunter's truck and driving away. Before he charged headlong into the fray, the thought crossed his mind. But then, he remembered the freaks had taken the bodies of Hunter and his accomplice with them. And since the truck wasn't running, he figured the keys were with the corpses. He would die of exposure before long, so while he still had some warmth left in him, he decided to kill as many of the freaks as possible. If he could do enough damage, it might allow Skylar to escape if she was still alive.

When he saw her nude and alive, he had a renewed sense of hope. But when the army of mutants poured out of the house, he knew he was fucked.

His thigh was on fire. Warm blood soaked his pants, and it felt like he pissed himself. The cold was clawing its way deeper into him, but a chill came from within.

Holding the spear in his hands like he was warding off a pack of wolves, Emmett swiped at the closest mutant, scraping a freakish girl's hand.

She cried and whimpered, sounding like a child.

There was no remorse in Emmett's actions. He knew it was kill or be killed. He thrust at another, missing the creature.

This is it. I'm fucked.

Emmett saw stars when the club wielded by the mutant hit him on the forehead. He dropped in the snow again. His blood turned the white around him red.

The mutants swarmed him, and he closed his eyes, awaiting the death blow.

"Stop!" a loud voice yelled.

The mutants froze. Each of them looked at one another, confused, with crude weapons hanging from deformed hands.

It was the big one—the king freak who used the axe to kill his friends—the one who threw that same axe at Emmett as he ran into the woods.

"He's mine." The big freak trudged through the snow, kicking the powder as he did.

His crooked eyes locked on Emmett's. There was a look of hatred and death on the face of the freak. But

Emmett wasn't looking at the monster, but rather past it at the house.

In the window of the lit house stood Skylar.

***

Hammer stepped on the wounded boy's fingers as he reached for the spear. The boy wailed as Hammer ground the small bones into a bloody pulp under his boot.

Bending down, Hammer grabbed the screaming boy by his throat, immediately cutting off his yelps of pain. His massive hands closed tighter around the soft neck of the frightened teen.

The kid battered Hammer's arms with both his good and ruined hand, but to no avail.

Grunting as he squeezed, Hammer smiled as the soft muscle of the throat turned to mush under his grasp. Vertebrae snapped and popped as the light faded from the kid's eyes, but Hammer wasn't done. He increased the pressure, feeling his crooked fingers sink into the meat of the dead flesh. Blood flowed around his hands, and yet he squeezed.

The Runts cheered at Hammer's feet as the dead boy's head fell off.

Hammer let the corpse fall to the snowy ground. He bent and picked up the head, which was locked in a look of fear. Holding it like a trophy, he roared into the night sky.

CHAPTER 22

Skylar cried. She was the only one left and knew her death would come now that they'd killed Emmett.

The big freak held Emmett's head high, drinking the dripping blood that leaked from the stump of his neck. Gore ran down his mutated face as he lapped it up with glee.

A sound caught Skylar's attention. It was something odd and sounded out of place for such a hell hole: a baby crying.

"Who the fuck are you?" an elderly voice asked.

Skylar turned. She did her best to cover her nudity. Even in the dire situation, her modesty was instinctual.

A withered old woman with stringy gray hair and a face that had seen too much clutched a newborn to her chest. "Crow!" the old woman shouted, rushing to the dead mutant with the axe in his face.

She crouched down, her knees popping as she did.

The baby cried louder at the abrupt scream.

"You! You fucking did this." The old woman looked up at Skylar with tears in her eyes. "You and your fucking kind have wanted to kill us all, to wipe us out because we aren't *normal*." The woman wrapped the baby tight and set the screaming bundle on the floor away from the corpse of the mutant. "I'll fucking kill you!" The old woman stood and grabbed a mallet from the counter.

Skylar removed her hands from her breasts and vagina, allowing herself to face the attack. She raised her hands as the woman swung the mallet. A sharp pain vibrated through her forearm as the force of the attack slammed her arm into her face. She stumbled back, doing her best to keep her feet under her.

The heat of the fireplace singed her backside.

She turned, looking for something to defend herself with. Spotting an old rack holding fireplace tools, she grabbed the first thing within reach.

Pulling the poker free, she knocked the rest of the tools to the ground. They fell in a clash of metal, eliciting more cries from the baby.

Skylar dodged the attack from the old woman and swung the poker.

The flat end of the tool caught the woman in the face, dimpling her skull. She fell to the ground in pain, but wasn't out of the fight.

Rough voices echoed from outside. The rest of the mutants were back.

She looked at the door, expecting them to crash through at any second.

The elderly woman screamed, but the wet sound turned into laughter. It was the laugh of someone who knew they'd get the last blow.

Skylar turned, horrified at what she saw.

The injured woman was standing on shaky legs. Her hands sizzled and burned as she pulled a pot of boiling water from a hook in the fireplace. The black iron was tacky with melted flesh, but it didn't stop her from throwing it in Skylar's face.

The scalding water hit Skylar, causing her skin to redden and bubble instantly. The light went out from her left eye as the delicate tissue swelled and burst. Her left shoulder and breast blistered and hissed, further disfiguring her.

Skylar screamed. In her fury and pain, she swung the poker again. This time, the hook on the tool buried itself into the woman's neck. She ripped it free, sending a gout of arterial blood splashing against the wall.

The elderly woman flailed, putting her withered, burned hands to her neck, doing what she could to stem the flow. She stumbled and fell, landing in the fireplace.

Her gray hair ignited, as did her clothes. With her last ounce of strength, she rolled herself out of the flames, igniting a wicker chair.

"Grammy!" the massive mutant yelled as he rushed into the house.

Her skin was a mess, and she was blind in one eye, but Skylar could see well enough to detect the anger on the monster's face.

"You cunt!" he yelled as the flames licked the base of the wall.

Skylar held the poker in one hand, but her strength was waning.

Like a bull, the freak charged her. He had no weapon, not that one was necessary to kill her.

She saw what he did to Emmett with just his bare hands—hands that were red with her friend's blood. Lowering the tip of the poker, Skylar aimed it at the belly of the beast.

His momentum carried him forward and right into the tool, impaling himself.

Skylar fell to the ground, but at the last moment, the mutant turned, doing his best to avoid the deadly instrument. It was the only thing that saved her life.

The monster lay writhing in pain on the ground with the poker sticking up from his gut.

She needed to end him, but the smoke and heat were beginning to overwhelm her. Death was coming, but if she could kill the beast who slaughtered her friends and brother, it would be worth it.

Gripping the handle of the poker, Skylar pulled, but the hooked end was snagged on his innards. She squatted, using her legs to power her as she yanked.

The hook ripped free, and with it came a coil of the beast's intestines. Blood—black and stinking like shit—came with the hook. Spools of pierced gut unraveled like a pull in a sweater.

The mutant spat up blood, coughing it onto his face as the flames crept closer to him.

She released her grip on the poker and turned to run.

"Not so fast, you fucking bitch!" The mutant grabbed her ankle, holding her in place.

Black smoke filled the room, burning Skylar's eyes. Her entire body felt scorched, inside and out. She coughed and coughed. It felt like she'd throw up her lungs if she didn't leave the room soon.

Skylar grabbed the poker one last time and swung.

The heavy iron smacked into the freak's wrist, breaking bones and releasing his grasp.

She pulled away, and in his last dying act, swiped at her feet with his broken arm.

She was falling, and she knew once she hit the

ground, she'd never get up. Her body was tapped; the adrenaline was used up and gone. She was going to die in that house of horrors.

Her chin hit the ground. She bit through her tongue and cracked more than a few teeth. The darkness was closing in around her, but she saw something else: a pair of large feet.

Her world went black, and she felt weightless.

CHAPTER 23

Skylar's senses slowly returned. The tang of smoke invaded her nostrils. It was thick, and she could almost taste it. Next, a sound pierced her ears: a baby crying. Her eyes fluttered open, but something was wrong with the left one. Then, the pain arrived. Her body was in agony. Her left eye felt like it had been replaced with a hot ember.

There was a blanket over her, but each beat of her heart caused her scalded flesh to rub against the coarse material. She was still nude, but at least she was covered.

"Hey, she's awake. The bitch didn't die," a voice shouted.

Skylar looked up at the rough beams of the ceiling. Something, no some*one*, was perched above her.

It was a boy no older than nine. His face was pinched and looked like he'd swallowed something sour.

She didn't know if she was seeing double, even with one eye, but it appeared the boy had four arms, two on each side. He used his extra limbs to dangle from the beams and swing his way over to the post holding the ceiling up.

Heavy footsteps echoed off the wood as a crowd gathered around her.

No, no, no. The freaks! They kept me alive to torment me! She wept. The tears amplified the pain in her ruined eye.

Skylar looked up at the big freak. Not the murderous one she was sure she'd killed, no, this one was fat, tall, and eyeless. He had a slow ignorance about him, more beast than man, but that wasn't what she focused on.

The set of heavy tits that hung over his shoulders swung as the mutant on his back guided him to her bed.

"Ah, I see you didn't die, which is a damn shock, and good luck for all of us," the three-fingered girl said from astride her mutant.

"Please don't kill me," Skylar begged.

The girl laughed. "Hell, if we were going to kill you, we would've left you in the house to cook with the others. No, we don't kill our own."

"Our…own?"

The girl laughed. "George, find me a mirror or something shiny."

The four-armed boy scurried away. Moments later, he came back holding an old compact mirror.

The mutant girl opened it, showing Skylar her fate.

Skylar's face was a mess. Her left eye was puckered and red, weeping yellow pus. The rest of her face was raised with blisters, each pulsing with fluid. Half of her hair was gone, burned away by the scalding water and fire from the house.

"The rest of your left side is just as bad, and your

one titty looks like a rotten piece of fruit. No one in your world is gonna take you like that. But in our world, you'll fit right in. And you killed our mother, Grammy, and our leader, Hammer, so you have no choice. Help us, or we can kill you and see where we end up."

The baby screamed in the background.

"And we need someone to raise the new Runts. To nurture them and help them. Needless to say, not many of us are the nurturing type."

One of the Runts, another deformed girl, carried the baby over to Skylar's bed and gently lowered the swaddled infant onto her chest.

She took hold of the deformed baby with her right arm, holding it close.

It stopped crying and stared at her with a cute, yet mutated, face.

Skylar did her best to smile back, but her mouth had been burned as well. Her tongue felt thick, and she could taste blood. A piece of it was missing, as were a few teeth.

"So, what's it gonna be?" the mutated girl astride the even bigger mutant asked.

Feeling like she was trapped in a nightmare, Skylar nodded and instinctively bounced the baby, who was giggling and content.

"Welcome home, Raisin. My name is Bags," she waved a hand behind her, showing Skylar the rest of the mutated kids and adults, "and these are the Runts."

EPILOGUE

Kristina felt like she'd aged well, but having money could do that for a gal. Serums, surgery, and sleep were the three 'S's' that kept her looking young, at least in her mind. She was just about to turn fifty-six, and her life was quite a whirlwind.

Twenty-four years earlier, she thought the U.S. government would shut her down and throw her in prison, but thanks to a horny EPA executive, Kris avoided all of that.

Smart stock moves, accompanied by insider trading, helped her grow her chemical business into an empire.

After she created SKV092509, Kristina was more cautious about what she produced. The toxin was pure poison which probably wouldn't have been very profitable. She didn't mind making things that could kill or maim, but they had to make her money.

The day she saw what the chemical had done to the test rats, she knew it had catastrophic potential. But with the creation of Homeland Security, slipping it past the authorities would be more complicated than fucking the right person.

After a few real estate acquisitions and good investments, she brought KrisCorp to the forefront of business.

A new piece of waterfront property was rezoned after a few million dollars found the right pockets. The endangered snail species was the sticking point, but when the right people were paid off, they miraculously disappeared from the equation.

Kris, and some of her associates, spent millions to get the property rezoned without guaranteeing it would be purchased. But the saying 'scared money won't make money' rang true with her.

The gravel crunched under the tires of her Mercedes SUV as she pulled up to the property.

Other luxury cars were parked sporadically, along with a few work trucks likely belonging to contractors hired to scope the land.

Kristina checked her makeup one final time in the mirror before exiting the vehicle. The hem of her dress was just high enough to show off her toned legs, but still low enough to exude class. A rope of clear diamonds adorned her lithe neck, with a matching set of earrings dazzling in the early sunlight.

It was a perfect spring day; if she played her cards right, she could break ground by the end of summer.

She had it all mapped out in her mind—forty luxury condos with lakefront views. Her little piece of heaven would rent out for almost $5k per unit, giving her another avenue of passive income, further building her empire.

The land was entrusted to the Goldwell/Stark Real Estate Company. Even though she had purchased many plots of land, Kristina hadn't dealt with Goldwell/Stark yet, but she'd heard stories about their top broker, Louise Havison.

Louise was in her early seventies, but still sharp in business dealings, or so Kristina heard.

The picture of Louise on the Goldwell/Stark website showed a no-nonsense woman with a head of sharply-styled gray hair, and a body that had birthed a child or two.

Men and women Kristina had dealt with her entire career flocked toward her.

She ignored them, seeking out Louise, who was standing at the edge of a lake with a man in work clothes.

Walking over to the pair, Kristina got their attention with the sound of her high heels grinding away at the gravel underfoot.

Both of them turned to look at the stunning woman.

The contractor's eyes quickly looked her up and down before he excused himself. "Ladies," he said, with a quick nod before walking back to a group of working men.

"Hello, Mrs. Havison, I'm Kristina Tropiano." She extended her hand, which the older woman grasped.

For a woman in her seventies, Louise had quite the grip. "Actually, it's *Miss* Havison," she said with just a touch of scorn.

Am I imagining things, or does this bitch already hate me?

Kristina had a reputation in the business world, so there was a good chance the older woman already had a preconceived notion about her. It was her job to smooth over the prejudice Louise had and secure the property.

"Oh, okay, *Miss* Havison."

"I've been divorced for almost twenty years and couldn't keep my husband's name any longer. You might recognize it. Briggs. Does that ring a bell?"

The malice was all but physical now.

Kristina felt the first bead of sweat trickle between her cleavage. "Clay Briggs? He used to be an executive member of the EPA."

Louise clasped her hands together. "You should remember him quite well considering you two used to fuck all the time."

And there it was.

Clay would never bring his wife to conventions, and now Kristina could see why. This old bitch probably never put a cock in her mouth and was, almost certainly, a dead lay. No wonder Clay divorced her.

"Oh, ah," Kristina stammered, trying to figure out how to get out of this mess.

Louise put a hand up, stopping Kristina's half-formed thought. "Save it, you fucking slut. I can't tell you how long I've been waiting for this day. For the day when I could hurt you like you hurt me and my family. This," she waved her hand at the pristine lake, "will never be yours. I will never let my boss sell to you as long as I still breathe. You can bet your fake tits on that."

Kristina was offended. She might use a little Botox here and there, but her chest was a gift from God—a gift that had been coated in Clay's spunk more than once.

"So, march your little ass back to your car and get the fuck out of here." Louise's neck was turning blotchy and red. The wrinkles around her mouth deepened with her frown and she looked on the verge of tears.

Having dealt with shrewd businesspeople her entire career, Kristina wasn't going to let someone stand in her way. She stepped closer, invading Louise's space.

The smell of perfume and cigarettes wafted off the older woman.

"We'll see about that." Kristina didn't say another word; she just turned and walked back to her car.

***

Louise looked out the dark window of her office. It had been a long, but rewarding, day. She received many great offers on the lakefront property, and her boss was more than happy. Her commission would be enough to fund her three-week-long trip to Europe, where she planned on seeing the sights, drinking too much wine, and possibly hiring an escort with a fat cock like the one her ex-husband had.

Thinking about Clay upset her, but seeing the look on Kristina's face when she dropped the hammer made it all the sweeter. She and Clay rarely spoke, especially since the kids were grown and moved across the country. She had no use for love anymore, and in her old age, sex was not something she needed much. When she felt the slickness of lust crawl over her, she took care of the urge with her vibrator.

She logged off her computer and locked it, then grabbed her purse and walked out of the empty building. She didn't mind staying late most nights; there wasn't much to go home to anyway. Her cat was self-sufficient, and all her favorite shows were streaming.

There was a liquor store on her drive, and she thought a bottle of wine, a bubble bath, and maybe a little fun with her sex toy was in order. She deserved it.

Louise walked through the dark parking lot. Her car was the only one left, parked under the lone streetlamp. But the lamp wasn't on, bathing the lot in darkness. The moon was full, but hidden behind thick clouds.

"Huh, that's strange," she said aloud as she walked to her car.

Glass crunched under her high heels. Thinking someone must've dropped a beer bottle in the lot, Louise paid it no mind. But she noticed more of it and realized it wasn't from a bottle. Looking up, she saw the shattered bulb of the streetlight.

Something moved in the darkness from the other side of her car—something massive.

A scream built in her throat as the clouds moved, allowing the moon to illuminate the monstrosity.

A monster stood before her—a man with horrid deformities. His face was shifted and distorted, making his flesh look like a Halloween mask. A cleft split his upper palate, showing jagged rows of teeth. His nose was wide and upturned, making him look more like swine than a man. Even his ears were wrong, misshapen, and hairy.

The freak stood almost twice Louise's height, and when she opened her mouth to scream, the beast jammed two fingers, each the size of a banana, into her throat.

He grabbed her lower jaw and pulled it down, snapping it free.

The sound of bone breaking and tendons tearing

echoed in Louise's ears. Before she could even mount a defense, paltry as it may have been, the freak slammed the back of her head into the light post. Her gray hair turned red as her skull fractured from each blow. A spurt of piss wet her tights and ran into her shoes as she died in a heap.

The mutant let her go and ran into the darkness.

***

Kristina sat with the engine running but the lights off. The alley was tight, but fit the car. It also gave her the perfect view of the carnage in the parking lot.

A shadow the size of a bear lumbered through the darkness, heading toward the car.

The dome light turned on as her son, Clayton, jumped into the passenger seat.

"I did it, Momma," he said with some trouble thanks to his pronounced cleft. "I killed her good, that bitch." Which sounded more like *bish*.

Kristina patted her son's strong hands. They were still wet with saliva and blood, but she'd clean him when they got home. Then, she'd read him a story and tuck him in. "I know, baby. You did good. Momma loves you." She put the car in drive, flicking on the headlights as she pulled out.

"Who was she, Momma?" Clayton asked.

She didn't have the heart to tell him the dead woman was his stepmother, not that he would have cared. She was the most important thing in his life, and he was the most important thing in hers.

"No one, baby. Put your headphones on and look out the window."

The freakish man did as he was told. He always

did.

Kristina unlocked her cell phone and dialed a number. It was late, but she knew her call wouldn't be ignored.

A groggy man answered on the other end of the line.

"Mr. Goldwell, this is Kristina Tropiano. I want to make you an offer on the lakefront property."

ABOUT THE AUTHOR

Daniel J. Volpe is the Splatterpunk Award-winning author of PLASTIC MONSTERS, TALIA, LEFT TO YOU, and many others. His love for horror started at a young age when his grandfather unwittingly rented him, *A Nightmare on Elm Street*. He can be found on Facebook @ Daniel Volpe, Instagram @ dj_volpe_horror , X @DJVolpeHorror , TikTok @danieljvolpehorror1

Runts

www.ingramcontent.com/pod-product-compliance
Ingram Content Group UK Ltd.
Pitfield, Milton Keynes, MK11 3LW, UK
UKHW020014050825
7227UKWH00001B/33

9 781961 758216